BEASTKEEPER

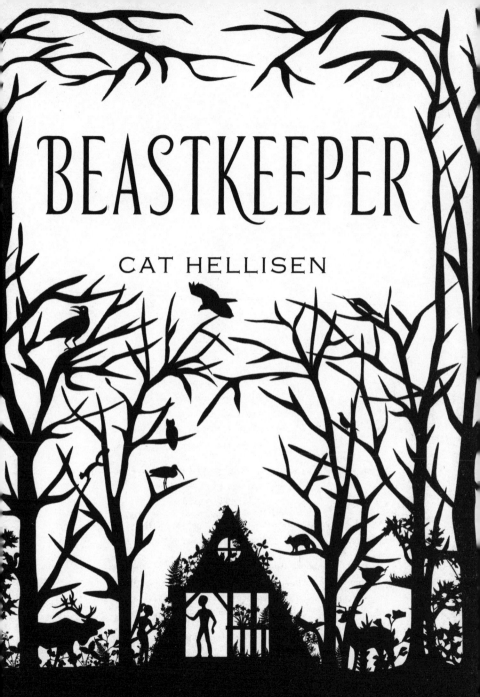

BEASTKEEPER

CAT HELLISEN

Henry Holt and Company
New York

Henry Holt and Company, LLC
Publishers since 1866
175 Fifth Avenue
New York, New York 10010
macteenbooks.com

Library of Congress Cataloging-in-Publication Data is available.
ISBN 978-0-8050-9980-5

Henry Holt books may be purchased for business or promotional use.
For information on bulk purchases, please contact Macmillan Corporate and
Premium Sales Department at (800) 221-7945 x5442 or by e-mail at
specialmarkets@macmillan.com.

First Edition—2015/Designed by Ashley Halsey

Printed in the United States of America by R. R. Donnelley & Sons Company,
Harrisonburg, Virginia

1 3 5 7 9 10 8 6 4 2

For my daughters, Noa and Tanith,
who both know there is always a cottage in the forest
and the beast is never just a beast

FLY AWAY, FLY AWAY

THE AIR WAS FULL of ice the night Sarah's mother packed all her bags and walked out. That was the thing Sarah remembered most. How it was so cold that the weathermen had said it might snow. She lay awake, listening for snow hushing against the roof—and instead she heard her parents arguing.

"I can't do this," her mother said. She was whispering so as not to wake her daughter. She never seemed to realize that Sarah was almost always awake. The smallest sounds could keep her from sleeping.

Sarah uncurled herself from her warm duvet, stretched out in the crisp air, and lay very still. Sometimes when she woke in the dark she would play little games with herself—games that she knew she should have already outgrown, so she never spoke about them to anyone. They were silly, childish things, and she knew enough to understand that there was no admitting to silly childish things when you were past a certain age. Sometimes in the dark she would pretend that she was a mouse, waiting for a snake to pass, and she would hold herself so still she could feel her own heartbeat vibrating her body. Sarah liked to think that night was the best time to work on staying silly and childish. Darkness always seemed more understanding about those sorts of things. More accommodating.

Tonight wasn't right for games, though. The night felt wrong, and it gave the unexpected cold a different bite, like a knife edge. It was the burr in her mother's voice, that sound of tears caught sticky in the throat—they gummed up her words.

Not good, Sarah thought. *The very opposite of good, in fact.* Softly, softly, she slipped her bare feet to the ground and padded to her door. Her toes were numb even against the springy wool of the carpet. She frowned and hugged her night-gown quickly around her. It hardly ever got this cold. And when it did, her parents would switch on the space heaters and keep the house warm enough to melt the butter on the bread.

Her mother hated the cold. Hated it fiercely. She gritted her teeth against it and would refuse to go outside if the temperature dropped. When winter came she cocooned herself in blankets and scarves, even as the heaters clicked and hissed the house warm.

Sarah opened the door to her room and peered out along the landing. The only light came from under her parents' bedroom door, and from a blue pool of moonlight under the small window at the far end of the passage. Her mother's voice was clearer now.

"I can't, Leon. I've tried—you know I have—but it's been long enough." Her mother sounded not so much sad as defeated. Sarah could picture her face, still and beautiful and expressionless. She was a woman who never let herself smile. Occasionally she would forget and the corners of her mouth would flit up for just one moment, and then she would remember herself, and her face would go calm and smooth as nothingness again. That was how she kept herself so very beautiful. Strong emotions leave their marks on a woman's face, she'd once said. "Never get sad, never get happy, never get angry."

But she was angry now, in a dull sort of way. Angry enough that Sarah could imagine the faintest lines of a frown pinching the skin of her mother's forehead.

"We'll move," her father said. His voice was rough, thick and choked up as tangled fur. "Someplace warmer—we'll go to the tropics—"

"It's not about the weather," her mother said. There was a thud. "Just hold this closed so I can get it—" A snap and a click. The sound of bags being struggled shut.

As if her mother were going on vacation to someplace with palm trees and colored fish that hung like ornaments in the slowly rising walls of the waves.

"Then what is it about?" But Sarah could hear that he already knew.

Sarah had discovered that while she liked to ask questions in the hopes that someone or other could answer them, adults liked to ask questions they already knew the answers to. She wasn't sure why exactly that was, and had finally decided that as people grew older, the more important something was the easier it became for them to forget. They had to keep asking as a way to help them remember.

There was a long silence, drawn out and stretched like a strand of bubblegum.

Sarah tiptoed along the landing toward her parents' room and wondered what flavor silence was, and if it grew hard and brittle if you threw it away, or if people sometimes stepped on wads of discarded silence and it stuck to the soles of their shoes and made their footfalls softer.

She stepped on the silences, and padded fox-quiet.

"I have to go," her mother said, instead of answering her father's question. "I can't stay and watch us falling apart, and watch it happening."

"You know what waits for you if you walk out of here. You can't just—"

A closet door banged, and then her mother's voice came soft, tired. "I know, Leon. That's why I'm leaving. Better that than to sit and watch you turn, to know there is nothing I can do to stop it." She took a gasping breath, and when she spoke again her voice had a thick sound, clogged up with tears. "And to know that one day the same thing is going to happen to my little bear . . ."

Sarah paused. They were talking about her. Her mother expected something to happen to her, and a fiddlehead of apprehension unfurled in her chest.

"You're a coward."

She'd never heard her father say anything like this to her

mother. Even when they did fight, he always withdrew himself, like a monster into a cave, and left her mother to work her own way through whatever had upset her. Sarah wondered how her mother would respond to this accusation.

Her mother only said, "I have been many things in my life. Now I choose to be something else."

"This is madness," her father said, but there was a serrated panic under his words. "You can't do this," he said. "There's no coming back. Please. You can't—"

The door swung inward, and Sarah was staring into her mother's face, which was still and cold as the night and unmarked by sadness or anger or hurt. If Sarah hadn't heard the tears in her voice earlier, she would have had no idea that her mother felt anything at all—until Sarah looked into her eyes, the only things that gave her away.

"Sarah." Her mother's dark eyes gleamed bird-bright. She looked like a small animal caught in the headlights of a car— half terrified and half resigned to its death.

Sarah had never seen her like this, not in all the winters she could think of. And winters were when her mother was at her worst, her love at its most brittle.

Her mother swallowed, began to stammer something, then shook her head, the fear fading from her eyes and being replaced by a glassy blankness instead. "You should be in bed. It's late, and it's cold out." She stepped past Sarah and went down the unlit stairs, the tail of her winter-blue coat flapping about her calves, her matching scarf wound tight around her throat like she was trying to stanch a wound, her bag thumping after her on its ridiculous little wheels.

"Merete," her father said, but her mother never even looked back at the sound of her name.

After the door had closed—gently, because Sarah's mother hardly ever slammed things—her father sighed and rubbed one hand across his chest like he'd eaten too fast. His face twisted, just once, a terrifying snarl of despair and rage, and then it was smooth again.

He was also dressed, though it was late. They'd been up the whole time, Sarah guessed, having an argument as chilly and quiet as the stars themselves. "Your mother's right," he said, as if she had not just walked out the door. He smoothed his heartburn out of his chest. "It's cold. Go back to bed— we'll talk about all this in the morning."

"I can't go back to sleep now." Sarah said the words very slowly, worried that she'd somehow startle this man, this father who wasn't acting a thing like her father. He didn't even care that his wife had just walked out in the middle of the night. Had she left him? Left *her*. "I can't—" She pointed down the stairs instead, waiting for the flood to build up. Her heart was fluttering, *hurting*, it was beating so fast. "Mom just packed and walked out of the house, and you want me to go to bed? Is she going to be all right? What happened? Do you know where she's going?" The questions tumbled over themselves trying to get out of her mouth.

"The power must have tripped," her father said, as if he hadn't even heard Sarah at all. "That's why the heaters went." He flicked the hall light switch up and down to show her, though Sarah didn't care. She'd always been able to see well in the dark. Then her father coughed. It was a hard, tearing noise, like he was going to rip apart right before her eyes. The coughing fit shuddered all down his body, shaking his bones about.

For a moment Sarah thought it might be all the tears he was trying to pretend weren't inside him, but when she reached out to touch his shoulder he pushed her hand away.

As the coughing finished, her father straightened again, eyes streaming and one hand still clutched over his mouth like he was frightened he was going to cough up his own lungs. Without speaking, he raced down the stairs.

Sarah's heart soared right up into her throat. He was going to burst out into the night and call her mother back. It had just been a stupid little fight that had gone a step too far, and now it was over, and her father would draw her mother back into the warm nest of home, and they would all go to sleep, and this would be a bad dream. Just tangles to be brushed away in the morning.

There was a clicking from downstairs in the kitchen, and the hallway light flooded on. The house—which had been re- markably silent—began its regular whir and hum.

Her heart plunged back down, and Sarah stared at her toes, frozen nubs in the deep blue of the hall carpet.

Around her, the air began to warm.

Sarah wondered if she should run after her mother— running was, after all, the only thing she was really good at, the only thing that ever got her noticed at school or after school. But her feet, which could strike the earth so hard, push her through the air like a racing deer—they seemed now to be weighted with lead, too heavy to lift, sinking her into the ocean of the carpet.

⁺⁺ ➤·· ⁺⁺

Her parents had always moved around a lot. Partly it was because of her father's work, but her mother had called it sun-chasing, so Sarah knew there'd been more to it than just following the money. Not that there was very much money. Her mother normally worked from home, sewing clothes and making alterations, and her father went off to do whatever it was that fathers did. He'd always come back smelling like metal and diesel, and he would wash his hands with a special, strong soap-cream that her mother bought in bulk. He would clean under his nails and around them, grooming himself with catlike fastidiousness before he would come to dinner.

Sometimes Sarah would sit on the edge of the bath and talk to him while he picked his nails clean. She would ask, "Why do you have to take so long? It doesn't take me that long."

"Somehow, I don't think going to school leaves you quite as filthy as my job does."

And Sarah would say, "Shows what you know," and her father would laugh and say, "Indeed."

When she looked at the weirdness of her parents compared to her classmates' parents, it would make her feel a little bit better to know that at least her mother and father's sole ambition in life wasn't just to make money, money, and more money. They didn't have a shiny new car and expensive clothes or a big house with rolling green lawns.

And it didn't matter, because her parents were at least interesting. They did things. They packed up when they got bored and they left, like migrating swallows. They weren't tied down to their fancy cars and heirloom furniture. It was one of the things she told herself every time the plastic storage containers came out of the garage, every time the contents of her home were packed away and labeled. It was that or let the sinking feeling take over and pull her feet-first into the ground and bury her.

Sarah had made herself become used to changing schools. She could even tell the signs: when the wind turned, and the first acorn caps began gathering in the gutters. When the martins skimmed and wheeled and patterned the sky with their dances, she would know that the move was coming soon.

She would know to gather her library books and turn them in.

It wasn't always seasonal. It was just a knowing. Sometimes she'd be walking home from school, kicking the grass, and a dandelion head would burst and scatter just so. The seeds would drift up in front of her, and from the geometry of their flight she would know.

When she got home, her mother would be sorting all their life into boxes.

Sarah never went out of her way to make friends anymore, or stand out in her classes. She made sure she was an adequate student and would spend her breaks catching up on the work she'd missed.

When you're constantly changing schools, there's always work to be caught up. Her only confidants were the toys she still kept, and they never told her that everything was going to be all right. They would just look at her glassily and smile their tight-sewn smiles.

✦⊹ ➤··⊰ ⊹✦

All this meant was that the next morning, Sarah got up and went to school, and no one knew her mother had flown away, had left her and her father alone in the boring rabbit-hutch house they were renting at the moment. For the other kids in her class, nothing had changed.

Sarah tried to pretend that they were right, that nothing really had changed. *If I believe it hard enough . . .* she thought to herself, but didn't give in to completing the wish. That way, if it didn't come true, she wouldn't feel that double slap of disappointment. That not only was her mother gone, but also there was no magic in the world.

In the books that Sarah liked to read, children who had to move around a lot seemed to always end up in strange houses with extra doors that went to new lands, tunnels and connecting passages, or boarded-up rooms that held treasures, ghosts, mysteries. Old houses filled with secrets and strangeness, gardens tangled up with adventures. The reality was that every house Sarah had ever moved into had been almost exactly the same. It was true that some of them had been single-stories with big gardens, others had been double-stories, some had neat little squares of lawn, and others had gravel driveways or concrete backyards, but the essence of the houses had always been the same. They were all clean and modern, with enough plugs to satisfy her parents, built-in cupboards, and neat kitchens with all the conveniences expected of them.

It's hard to find magic in houses like that. And Sarah wanted magic, wanted to know that there was something more to her life than packing up and moving, and going to new schools, and not bothering to learn the names of the people around her because what did it matter, really.

The first day after her mother fled, Sarah held on to her hope that this was just temporary and that she'd be back before the week was out. But there was no mother that day. Or the next. Or the next. The little hope shriveled up and fell away, and Sarah swallowed down that ugly, salty taste in her mouth and held her head higher. She let the sky lick her eyes dry and the wind kiss her welcome.

Her father went to work as if nothing had changed, and the boxes gathered dust in the garage. Sarah almost wanted to come home one day to find him packing up the house, because at least that would be something normal. Or if not packing, then looking for her mother, even if it meant printing up posters of her mother's startled face in black and white, with a phone number and a reward offered. Although Sarah wasn't sure that would exactly work for getting back a parent.

Instead, the laundry gathered in the baskets and overflowed, the dust bunnies multiplied under the beds and couches, the cutlery tarnished, the weeds grew in the gutter alongside the house. Sarah discovered that untended houses very quickly give in to neglect. She'd never understood how much her mother had done while she'd been in class and her dad was at work. She'd always sort of assumed that the places just looked after themselves.

Reality was very different, Sarah realized, after using the last of the clean dishes for the dusty remains of the very last box of cereal. Her father had stopped eating, had seemed to forget that children needed food.

"We need groceries," Sarah said to him that night over a boiled potato gone mushy on the outside but still woody in the middle.

Her father was dressed in his stained blue overalls and watching television. His hands and clothes left inky smears over the fabric. Under his ragged nails, the dirt gathered black. When he turned at the sound of her voice, there was a flash of something in his eyes, an empty green flare. He was unshaven, and his beard bristled over his face, like he'd glued clippings from a doormat all over his cheeks and chin. "Hmm," he said, but he reached into his pocket to pull out his worn leather wallet and peeled out some crumpled notes for her. They were as grubby as he was. Her father held them out, and Sarah slipped down from the chair and padded over nervously to take them.

He smelled odd, musty and sour, like a sick dog caught in the rain.

But she'd been able to buy bread and apricot jam and peanut butter and instant noodles, so at least she didn't have to starve.

2

AN IMPROBABLE BOY

AFTER A WHILE Sarah gave up hoping, and when she walked home along the grassy pathways, she held on to her disappointment instead. It was all she had. She would recite a new mantra to herself, and let it fill her head. That way she could feel like she was Dealing With It, and other things that grown-ups did.

After all, there is nothing quite like losing a parent to knock the childishness out of a person's spirit.

The freak icy snap had passed, and the weather had gone back to being the usual cold and sunny days interspersed with mushy drizzle. Sarah was on her way home from school, and the late-afternoon sun slanted thinly down through a clean blue sky tufted with the faintest wisps of faraway clouds.

Her bag was slung over one shoulder. It was so overladen with books that the thin strap dug right through her school blazer and made her shoulder ache. It pulled her whole body off center. As she walked, she kicked at the pathway, and in her head the disappointment mantra was on a loop: *Dad-and-I-are-all-alone*-kick-*Dad-and-I-are-all-alone*-scuff.

It was better to repeat this over and over in her head until it stopped making sense than to give her mind space to start hoping again.

Every now and again her thoughts would slip from her little singsong, and Sarah would catch herself just about to think that maybe when she got home, her mother would have flown back and would greet her at the door, would allow herself to smile, hug Sarah so hard that her ribs would break—

You are being ridiculous, Sarah thought. *You are being ridiculous.*

She was so busy repeating this to herself in the hope that she'd eventually believe it, that at first she didn't notice the boy following her.

If the house that Sarah and her father lived in now was as empty of magic as a broken wand, it still had one tiny redeeming feature. Between the school and her house lay a very small parcel of untouched land. It had a FOR SALE sign older than Sarah, and this sign leaned dejectedly on one overgrown corner. The words were faded away so that only close up could Sarah make out the faint shadows of what was written. The edges of the board were chewed ragged by rain and time.

Once, she supposed, the land had been cleared and ready

for someone to grow a house from its broken stones, but it had been left untended for so long that it had become something that was not quite a forest.

It was a thick tangle of fast-growing shrubs, and flowering weeds, and abandoned junk. The route through the Not-a-Forest was the long way to her house, but Sarah preferred to walk the extra distance on the narrow track that wound between the wiry bushes than to keep to the strict pattern of the roads.

Her parents had told her she must never walk that way, as people could be hiding in the bushes just looking for a girl like her to steal, and the warning had made her all the more determined to take that path.

Especially now.

It wasn't that she wanted anyone to steal her; it was more that she had long ago discovered a delicious pleasure in not listening to what adults say.

In all the times she'd taken the path, she'd never seen anyone else, anyway, which just went to show. She always saw *signs* that other people had been there—new litter, carvings in the bushes that had grown big enough to look almost like stunted trees, the stamped-out coals of cooking fires—but always it seemed to Sarah that the moment she set foot on the path, the Not-a-Forest became hers and everyone else fled.

That day, though, someone was in her realm and moving, silent, through the shrubs and weeds and rusted junk. Sarah paused to lower her bag to the ground so she could shake out her aching shoulder. It was only because of this that she stopped her little mantra and began to notice the world around her properly. Everything felt subtly wrong. It was as if a very neat thief had ransacked her forest and left only the smallest clues behind. The shadows had been moved an inch out of place, the bushes put back in not quite the right positions.

Sarah had a skin-prickling feeling that someone was watching her. She swung around in the middle of the path, looking in every direction, but saw no one.

"Who's there?" The birds and the rustling lizards went about their business, and above, the sky stayed cold and blue. Sarah swallowed. "Hello?" she tried again. She was starting to feel foolish now. "And maybe it's nothing," she said to herself as she bent to pick up her overstuffed bag.

"Maybe it's a murderer," said a stripling boy. He stepped out from behind a scraggly gathering of young eucalyptuses and pushed his russet-brown hair back from his forehead. "Or a hunter."

He was older than she was—he had that skinny, half-starved look that some boys got when they grew too fast for their meals.

A shiver went down Sarah's back, and she tightened her grip on her bag. She could run. She was fast. But perhaps not fast enough to outrun a lanky teenage boy. She kept her voice loud and firm even though at first the words felt shivery in her mouth. "Or maybe it's just some stupid high school kid," she said. Sarah wasn't far from high school herself, but she didn't quite trust the ones who had Moved On. The battle lines were firmly drawn, as far as she was concerned.

The boy frowned. "I don't go to school," he said. "I'm Alan. Who are you, then?"

Sarah had been warned never to speak to strangers, and this happened to be one of the adult rules that had managed to get itself stuck in her brain. Her parents hadn't explained just how strange a stranger had to be to make him really a stranger, but she was quite sure that this boy qualified. Names meant nothing.

He was dressed in thick corduroy trousers the color of bark and fallen leaves, the knees of which were black with dirt. His sweater was a gloomy green, like the middle of a pine forest, and he wore no shirt under it. In the thin and sandy soil, his bare feet were dirty as a child's, and around his neck he wore a necklace strung with dull ivory shapes. Teeth. Teeth of all kinds, all shapes. "Beast got your tongue?" he said.

"It's 'cat.'"

The boy crouched down in the long, pooling shadows of the young eucalyptus trees and clicked his tongue. He appeared to be looking at markings in the earth. "What is?"

"The saying. It's 'Has the cat got your tongue?'" Sarah eyed him. He was very definitely *off*, but at the same time he exuded a feeling of contentment. It crept up around Sarah, as soothing as her mother's whispers in the dark. She shrugged her shoulders like she was trying to shake off a too-heavy blanket. The feeling didn't go; it just pressed down, got even heavier, thicker. An eiderdown of warm laziness.

"Well, has it?" he said, and glanced up at her, one eyebrow raised.

Sarah leaned forward, just a little, as if to get a better view of whatever it was he found so fascinating on the ground. She'd listened to the girls in her class giggling over pictures they'd cut from magazines and stuck into their school notebooks, but she'd never understood why they got so *excited* over the actors and musicians whose faces covered the pages where their homework should be. She thought she might be a little closer to some kind of understanding now. It felt ridiculous. "Has what?"

"The cat. Got your tongue." The boy sighed. "We're talking in circles. What are you doing here, cat-girl?"

"I'm walking home." Sarah straightened. "And I could ask you the same thing."

Alan blinked. He had heavy eyelids; they made him look sly and sulky but—and here was the stupid part, Sarah thought—in a good way. "Could you really? Go on, then."

For a moment, she really wanted to ask him just that, why he was in her Not-a-Forest, what he was doing there in a place that was *hers*. "You're impossible."

That made him laugh. It was just the smallest little slip of good humor, and he caught it quickly. "Hardly. I'm just improbable." He stood again and looked to the sky. "And lost. This isn't the right part of the forest at all."

"It's not even a forest."

"Just so." He frowned. "I could have sworn her trail led here. Still." He tapped two fingers to his forehead. "It-was-a-pleasure-to-make-your-acquaintance." Then he smiled, and his face changed, the sly look brushed away with the glint of his teeth. He looked awkward, out of place.

"Um, same. I think." But Sarah said the last to an empty space. Alan had disappeared.

Sarah stared at the stand of eucalyptus saplings. After a

moment, she reached out to push the branches aside, wanting to catch a glimpse of wherever he'd gone to hide himself. There was nothing—no one. He'd simply vanished.

The birds began calling to each other, high and loud, and a fat bumblebee the size of her thumb droned past.

"It's Sarah," she said to the trees. "My name is Sarah." *What a strange boy.* She wondered briefly whom he could have been following. Then she turned and hurried the rest of the way home, and didn't even care too much when she found the house empty as expected.

THE NOT-A-FOREST

FOR WEEKS AFTER that encounter, Sarah stayed on the lookout for Alan in her Not-a-Forest. Although she saw all the usual signs of people there, she didn't spot the russet-haired boy again. Every weekday she cut through the tangle of undergrowth and saplings, hoping for a glimpse of his muddy green clothes or a flash of tanned skin, but as the month dragged on, she began to think that she'd never catch sight of him again.

That perhaps, after all, he'd merely been some kind of waking dream.

On weekends she'd escape to the wilderness with her stack of library books. Even though Saturdays brought out the strangers and the rambling children and left the Not-a-Forest feeling more like a little scrap of land where people dumped their rubbish and less like something magical, she'd still make her way to the clump of trees where they'd met, settle herself down on an old camping blanket she'd taken out of storage, and read her books. She'd pack herself lunch, and always make an extra sandwich just in case.

The end of every long afternoon brought with it the same strange disappointment, doubled by the heavy realization that once again she was going to return to a house that stood empty, waiting for her with its unwashed sheets and its sink full of dirty crockery. Once again, it hadn't even been worth it. Sarah tried to make herself not think about the odd boy. The odd *vanishing* boy.

+{⸱ ⸱➤⸱⸱⸦⸱ ⸱}⸱+

You're as pathetic as them, Sarah told herself, thinking of her giggling classmates, the ones who were sneaking off to flea-market jewelry stands so they could get their ears pierced. *And even worse, you're going insane. You had an imaginary conversation with an imaginary person. Like you're five.*

It was the end of another boring school day, and she'd promised herself that this time she wouldn't go wandering off to the abandoned plot of land. Sarah let herself into the house with the key that her father had tied onto a length of string and slipped around her neck so that it wouldn't get lost, cleared a cleanish place on the kitchen counter, and made herself something to eat.

Every afternoon she had a sandwich, which always had the same thing on it—peanut butter—because her father still hadn't mastered the concept of grocery shopping. After that she would rush through whatever homework she had and make an attempt to clean some of the large collection of gunked-up plates and cups. That afternoon was no exception.

"Where do you even come from?" she accused the dishes as she scrubbed them. "It's not like we use this many plates." Her father was at least eating again, and had taken to preparing supper almost every night, but so far he seemed to be stuck on eggs and fries, alternating with takeout.

Sarah gathered a scattered collection of greasy boxes and shoved them into the overflowing trash.

It would be hours before her father came home from work, so she changed out of her school uniform and did a load of laundry. After all, she needed to do *something* to stop herself from just grabbing a library book and heading out to the Not-a-Forest. Or worse, sitting at the window and watching and waiting and *hoping*.

Sarah curled up on one of the pin-striped couches in the front room, reading over her class notes and half listening to the whir of the machine. It was only when she got up to make herself a cup of tea that she realized things had gone badly wrong. She swung her feet down, and they landed in soggy carpet with a splash.

She froze. Cold water soaked into her socks. With a small "oh no," she looked down and stared at her feet. The white socks were now gray. The machine had flooded, and sudsy dirty water was slipping down the passage, drenching the carpets. "Oh. No."

Sarah lurched off the couch, abandoning it and her notes,

and slipped to the kitchen to turn off the water and the washing machine. It was too late, however. The kitchen was a shallow lake.

This was what being productive and helpful led to, Sarah thought as she splashed her way down the passage to fetch an armload of towels from the linen closet. She had to deplete the entire store, even the ones that were packed right at the back with little ornate soaps between them for freshness, before the worst of the flood was soaked up. The rest of the water she swept out the kitchen door.

"This is an epic disaster." Talking aloud was keeping Sarah from crying, but it wasn't doing a very good job. It seemed to her that there was no way to fix anything before her father came home. It wasn't like she could somehow vacuum all the water out of the sodden carpet. She toed the wettest part of the carpet, and the wool squelched at her.

It might, she thought, be worthwhile to take a very long walk, one that led her far away from the remaining mess. When she came back—no, *if* she came back—she would discover that none of it had actually happened, and the house wasn't a swamp of dirty water. She sighed. *As if.* Still, she thought it might be nice to pretend that could actually happen. Or perhaps that her dad would come home and clean the mess himself, after being racked with guilt over how Sarah was doing all the housework and he was doing nothing at all.

Now we're talking. Sarah hopped over the worst of the wet patches and the sudden new landscape of towel hills and woolly swamps, and went to grab dry socks and sneakers. A small pang of guilt squeezed at her as she locked the house behind her, but mostly she felt vast relief. And more than a smidgen of righteous fury—after all, why was this all falling to her? It wasn't fair. It wasn't fair that her mother had left them, it wasn't fair that her father was falling apart, and it wasn't fair that the only person she wanted to talk to didn't even exist.

Or probably didn't.

A few weeks ago Sarah had come up with the idea of leaving Alan a message. She hadn't really known what to write, and in the end had settled on a short note that read *What are you hunting?* and tucked the folded scrap of exam paper into a forked branch. It had stayed lodged there for several days, until it had finally disappeared. Sarah supposed that the wind had ripped it away, sent it tumbling over the shrubs and bushes.

If he was real, if he'd seen the note, then why had he never responded? Sarah cut through the overgrown little back alleyway that led out to the Not-a-Forest. The farther she got from the house, the more annoyed she felt. She refused to let herself worry about what was going to happen.

Let Dad clean up the house for a change. Let him shave, let him do the groceries, wash the dishes, and act like a human being, instead of this useless waste he's become. Sarah dashed a few hard, angry tears from her eyes and felt her throat close up tight from fury. *It's not fair.*

The season was hinting at change. Bracken was growing up around the thin, dark stems of the trees, and bare branches were just beginning to shimmer greenly. Even the sun seemed closer. Sarah squinted at the black trees. It was warm out here— the sun had baked the ground, had curled the edges of the arum lilies' broad leafy hearts.

Sarah went back to the section of pathway near the eucalyptus saplings and sat down in a patch of shade. She swallowed until the tight feeling in her chest began to soften and her shoulders dropped. A hazy contentment drifted over her as she leaned back against the biggest of the trees and watched the wind blow the new leaves of the tangled weeds with their pale purple trumpets. When she heard the softest crackle of dried leaves behind her, Sarah spun around, already in a crouch, ready to push herself up and away into a run.

A sun-browned face stared down at her, and Sarah wasn't sure whether to greet him like a lost friend or be angry at him for disappearing in the first place.

"Ah, the cat-girl." Alan squatted down so that his nose was level with hers, eyes wide. "Are you leaving me notes in the bushes?"

"Maybe." Sarah relaxed, but not completely. It felt like someone had just emptied a bowl full of goldfish straight into her stomach. They fluttered inside her, making her feel eager and ill at the same time.

"Why would you do that?"

She felt her face go red. "I was curious."

"And you know what happens to curious cats," said Alan. He drew his finger slowly across his throat and made an exaggerated *ghhh* noise.

"My dad says satisfaction brought it back," Sarah countered. She wasn't scared. Despite the kinda-sorta-almost death threat. It was hard to be scared around Alan. Whatever he said about being a hunter, he reminded her more of some cautious deer, with too-knobby legs and an awkward curiosity.

"Now, see, that's a lie. Dead beasts stay dead. There's no witchery that brings them back. Ailing beasts, on the other hand . . ." Alan half-shrugged. "As to your question, I'm hunting a bird, a little wren." He held his thumb and forefinger a few inches apart. "About so big."

"Is it rare?"

"Not very." Alan settled down on the ground, cross-legged. His bare feet were flecked with broken leaves and grains of rich dark earth like crumbs of chocolate cake. "It's finding the right one, you see."

"What happens when you catch it?" Sarah wasn't sure if she actually wanted to know. "You don't eat it or anything, do you?"

Alan frowned, and stared at her sidelong. "That's a funny sort of mind you have, cat-girl. I'm no beast. No." He sighed. "She's sickly, doesn't know what she's doing now, the little feather-brain. I need to find her so I can take her home and back to where she'll be safe. She flew away, and there's a woman pining for her. Pining so hard her heart is broken."

"Over a bird?" Sarah couldn't keep the amused disbelief out of her voice.

"Why not?" He looked away from her, toward the bushes, as if he might spot the flown-away bird eavesdropping on their conversation. "People find all sorts of things to love."

"Is that what you do—find missing pets?"

"Most times." Alan was still frowning. "I don't always find them in time, mind. Sick ones I can help, but if it's too late . . ." He drew a spiral in the soil with his index finger. There was black dirt ground under his nail. Tiny bright leaves like bracelet charms had caught in his hair, and Sarah wanted to comb them out, watch them fall. "There are times when it's better to put a beast out of its misery. I don't like it much, but there it is. Some truths are hard ones. Your father is bellowing for you."

"Huh?" Sarah looked around, though she could hear nothing more than the soft sound of the wind rustling through the branches, stippled over with bird calls.

"Listen," Alan said, and then Sarah could hear it, faint under the sighing wind. Her father *was* calling for her. She shouldn't have been able to hear him from so far away.

He was probably furious. Sarah went cold, then hot, then cold again.

"No need to be so scared. He's opened all the windows and the water is drying up. It'll be like old bones by morning." Alan was scrutinizing his fingers now, and cleaning under his nails with a splinter of white wood.

"Are you a wizard?" It sounded ridiculous the moment the words left her mouth, though not that ridiculous, she thought, considering. Alan was rather strange and fey, and if anyone was going to be magic, it would be this barefoot teenager with silver leaves caught in his hair. A boy who was hunting for a sick bird.

Alan shook his head. "Not a wizard, not as such, but I understand magic. And there's magic in forests. Even in yours," he said. "It's just a little piece of forest, but it remembers being part of the great old forest, and when you're in it, you remember too."

"Remember?" She couldn't understand a word of what he

was saying; it was like he was having a conversation with her, but she was saying the wrong things, all out of time. "Alan? Remember what?" But again Alan had slipped away like a shadow behind the sun. Her father's voice drifted over the roofs of the nearby buildings, and Sarah got to her feet, dusting the rich earth from her jeans. He was home earlier than she'd expected, and Alan seemed sure he wasn't angry about the washing machine disaster. Maybe that meant good news. She didn't let herself hope too hard.

⋅⊱ ⟶⋅⋅⟵ ⊰⋅

"Care to explain what happened?" Her dad was half smiling when he said it. At least she wasn't in serious trouble, then. Her mood lightened for a moment. Things weren't so bad. They'd get through it. Until she realized that his eyes were sad and hopeless. She thought she preferred it when he seemed half wild and dirty.

Sarah slipped onto one of the high bar stools that lined the kitchen counter. "It was an accident."

"No. It wasn't. There's someone to blame," he said.

Her hands were folded tightly on the counter. Sarah could see a tiny spike of nail sticking out like a splinter on one thumb. The skin around it had gone red and puffy where she'd chewed at the split.

"Me." Her father sighed. "You look as if you're expecting a thrashing or something. I don't hold you responsible, you daft thing." He curled his hands around hers. They were warm and a little sweaty, like he was running a fever. The hair on the back of his wrists looked thicker than it usually was, longer and darker. "Don't worry, Sarahbear, I'm going to do better, you'll see. Things will go back to normal."

How normal did he expect their lives to be? Was *she* coming back?

Sarah dragged her gaze away from the thick dark hairs on her father's wrists and met his eyes. They were shining. Candle-bright. He smiled, and his teeth were yellow, the gums receding so that they looked almost like lengthening fangs. "Trust me, Sarahbear."

A cold feeling swarmed up her arms. Ants made of frost were marching under her skin. "Okay," she said, even though she felt numb inside. "Okay."

4

THE DISAPPEARING ACT

"YOUR TEACHER WANTS a meeting with me," her father said. It was evening, several weeks after what Sarah privately referred to as the Washing Machine Incident. Sarah had no idea when her father had last showered. He'd called in sick today, she knew. He'd been here when she got back from school, sitting on the couch watching talk shows. He'd hardly spoken to her, hadn't even looked at her, like she was some kind of ghost that drifted through the house.

Sarah knew he wasn't sick. Or maybe he was, but not in the kind of way that meant sniffles and tissues and cups of hot water with lemon and honey. Her stomach swooped and dipped, and for a moment she could taste sour fear lodged in her throat. There were several reasons she could think of why her teacher would want to meet with her father now.

I'm dead. She was pretty sure she'd failed the last set of tests. And there was that thing where she'd missed a few days. Just a few. *It's not like we were learning anything new.* It was near end of term, and the exam cycle was over. People were just mucking around and getting ready to go on vacation.

So she'd taken some . . . days off. That's all they were. Sarah had spent them in the Not-a-Forest, wondering about Alan and the things he'd said to her about forests and what they remembered, and—most of all—hoping that she'd see him again. She looked for birds that were *so big*, sick ones, because if she found the wren, then she'd have a reason to leave him another note.

"Oh?" Sarah busied herself with her fried egg, mushing the yolk into bright yellow smears.

"She said that you've been sick quite a lot these last few weeks."

Her ears were burning. Sarah stared resolutely at her toast, watching the spilled yolk spread across the plate. *So dead.* She wondered what happened to girls like her. Next year was supposed to be the start of eighth grade, and then moving on to high school. And just moving on, probably, because that's what her family did. Maybe this time she'd end up in a reform school. *Stop being ridiculous. They do not send people to reform school for skipping a few—or more than a few—days. You have to at least stab someone. Or something.* Sarah stabbed her egg with the fork, and wondered if that would be enough, if she pretended it was whichever teacher had gotten in touch with her father. She ate, forcing the food into her mouth even though she wasn't hungry anymore and the egg was too cold and tasted of wobbly bland nothing. At least with her mouth full, she wouldn't have to talk.

"You forged my signature," her father added, his voice throaty, like a cat's growl. "I'm slightly impressed. It's not the easiest one in the world to copy."

The food got stuck, and Sarah had to swallow and swallow to make it go down. "Um," she said. "I *was* sick. I just didn't want to bother you."

Her father sighed. When he didn't say anything for a long time, Sarah glanced up. He was leaning his elbows on the table, his head in his hands. His shoulders were shaking, just the tiniest bit, but the strange shivering made her whole stomach knot up like old shoelaces.

He was crying. Fathers never cried. *Her* father never cried. Sarah pushed what was left of her dinner away from her. "I'm sorry." The words fell out onto the table and flew away like dandelion seeds, never reaching him.

"I'm not doing well by you," he said, not lifting his head. "This is no way for you to grow up. I need to go to . . . a special kind of hospital, and you need to go to people who can take care of you properly." He wasn't looking at her, as if he was lying and knew she'd see it.

"What?" The word burst out, startled. Sarah's stomach twisted and tightened; for a moment she thought she was going to be ill and puke up little gobbets of egg white and ketchup and chewed-up toast right onto the tabletop. "You're sending me away? Where? To who?"

She hadn't really been worried about reform school; that had just been her hyperactive imagination. It hadn't registered that her father might really want to get rid of her. Did he hate her that much? Maybe it *was* her. What this was all about. Why her mother had left, why her father was slowly going mad—it was her. She swallowed the thought down, and a fierce little voice in her head tried shouting that she was just imagining things, that it had nothing to do with her. But a louder, calmer voice smothered it. *My mother left, and the night she left, she was talking about how she couldn't deal with it. With me.*

And now . . .

Now her father was saying the same thing with different words, his face still buried in his hands.

A hiccuping sob jumped in her chest. Sarah could feel the tears choking up her throat. "You can't do that!"

But he could. So maybe it wouldn't be reform school—but there were other places. She had visions of herself sent off to a children's home or to some ancient aunt she'd never even known existed. "This isn't happening," Sarah said. It couldn't be. It wasn't fair. She'd lost her mother to the cold and the winds, and now her father was also lost, lost to some strange sickness that ate away the inside of his head until he wasn't anything like her father at all, just a beast wearing his skin like a coat. "I'm not listening to you."

Her father carried on talking through his fingers, talking and talking like if he stopped he'd have to realize how scared she was. "I'm sending you to your grandparents," he mumbled. "You'll be safe with them. They've wanted to see you for so long, and they—they're not bad people. A little strict, and maybe a little odd, but they love you very much—"

Grandparents? He was going mad, that was it. Or this was all some big unfunny joke he was playing on her. Something to scare her so she'd behave. And if these mythical grandparents had ever truly wanted to see her, why was this the first time her father had ever mentioned it?

"What grandparents?" Sarah shouted as she stood. "I thought all my grandparents were dead, and now you tell me, now you tell me . . ." Her knees shook. "I don't know what you're telling me," she said to the table. "You're a liar." Without looking at her father again, Sarah turned and ran from the house, out the kitchen door and into the dark wet of the night. She'd show him. He wasn't the only one who could frighten people.

The saw-toothed emerald grass in the alleyway slapped all around her legs, making her jeans heavy and damp. Above her the sky was deepest darkest blue, like the inside of a marble, and little tattered rags of dirty cloud stretched across the night. The moon was round and bright. It drowned out the stars and lit the alleyway and the distant trees of the Not-a-Forest.

Sarah raced down to the pathway and deep into the little lost parcel of abandoned land, to the place by the eucalyptus trees where she spent her time not-exactly-waiting to bump into Alan.

With the night had come the other owners of the land— the vagrants and the wanderers. Sarah skidded to a walk, her breath shuddering her ribs. Through the leaves and the slender trunks she could see the flicker of fire and hear the low voices of men and women.

The air was rich with wood smoke and raisin-sweet sherry. In winter, her mother had liked to have a sherry on the coldest nights, drinking it from a tiny, beautiful little glass that had made Sarah wish she was old enough to drink sherry too. The little curved glass had enchanted her. It was too good to be wasted on an adult.

The memories hit her, and all Sarah could do was stand there and let them batter her down. The feather-and-lily smell of her mother's hair, the sherries on cold nights, the watermelon summers, the sound of the bees humming around her mother while she gardened. The nights when her mother had still read to Sarah at bedtime from a book filled with myths and heroes. The way she almost never smiled, but when she did, it was small and secret and only for the person who had seen it, like when her dad told awful jokes and her mother would wink at Sarah just so and share that little twitch of her mouth.

There had been the Christmas Sarah had woken her parents in the dark and her mother had walked bleary-eyed to the tree and agreed that indeed Santa *had* already been, and that two o'clock in the morning was a perfectly reasonable time to drink hot chocolate and eat candy canes and unwrap presents. It had been so long ago, but Sarah could still remember the particular crisp and drying smell of the tree, the scatter-glitter of ribbons and discarded wrapping paper in reds and golds and greens. The feeling of sitting warm in her mother's lap, her mother's arms strong and protective, the sound of her unexpected laughter like the liquid call of a forest bird.

There were other, less happy memories. But they were still hers, still her mother in all her moods. The color of the shadows of her eyelashes across her cheeks as she sat next to Sarah's bed and watched Sarah through a fever, her hands clasped and bony.

The days her mother would sleep until noon and then spend the whole afternoon sitting at the kitchen table tearing junk mail into confetti. The other, worse days, when she stared out the window for hours, her fingers holding on tightly to her scarf. Nothing Sarah said on those days would make her so much as twitch in response.

Maybe those had been the signs that should have warned Sarah that the day would come when her mother would be actually gone—not just into some place inside her own thoughts, but for-real gone, with no intention of coming back.

Sarah sat down in the middle of the narrow track and sobbed into her palms.

The tears seemed endless, pouring hot and thick down her face. Her nose was running, and she was making little choking animal noises, sounds humans aren't supposed to make. The beast noises shook her body. Her skin felt less and less real, like a numb coating over the desperate, lonely little creature she really was on the inside. Sarah couldn't have stopped crying if she'd tried. There was just too much inside her, and now that she'd begun, it would be like trying to dam a flooding river.

She cried in the dark until the smell of smoke and sherry was drowned under salt.

After a while the sobs turned to hiccups and coughs and

splutters, and slowly, slowly, her shoulders stopped jerking so hard, and the worst of her sadness trickled out of her. She felt deflated. Sarah lowered her hands and wiped her sleeve across her face. Her eyes were tight and itchy. Inside she was empty and new, all cried out.

"Here," said Alan.

Sarah's head jerked up so quickly she felt something pull in her neck. "Gah!"

He was standing over her, frowning, a scrap of white material dangling from his fingers. "You should always carry a handkerchief."

Sarah grabbed at the piece of material and tried to cover as much of her face with it as she could. She was pretty certain that she looked more like a snot-nosed brat than anything else. "Thanks," she mumbled. "But no one normal uses handkerchiefs anymore."

"Are you saying I'm not normal?"

"Right, because normal people are always wandering around in the middle of the night, appearing and disappearing like a—like a ghost. Don't you have a home to go to?"

"What's wrong with handkerchiefs?"

"Nothing, I'm sure, if this was a hundred years ago." Sarah tried to laugh, but all she could feel was the horrible empty black space inside her. She was leaving, not because she wanted to but because *he* was sending her away. The man who called himself her father.

Alan crouched down so that his face was very close to hers. "Why were you crying, anyway?"

"Because." She wiped her face, scrubbing at it till her

cheeks felt raw, then handed the hankie back. "You wouldn't understand."

"Is that so?" Alan didn't stuff the material back into his pocket, but spread it out over his knee and began to fold it very neat and small. It was embroidered on one corner—*Freya*—in a swirly, curling script. "And why wouldn't I?" He tucked the folded hankie away.

"Because your mother didn't run out on your family, and your dad didn't go crazy, and no one's making you move, no one's making you leave and go to strangers—family you've never met. It's not fair."

"No." Alan stood and looked down at her. "I have no family to call strangers. And I live in a place where all that is left to me are the memories of the people I have loved. Is that better?"

Immediately Sarah's stomach did a slow, hideous somersault. "I—I didn't mean that. I'm sorry." She scrambled to her feet. "Where do you live? I mean, maybe I could—" *Not visit him, that would be ridiculous.* "I don't know . . ."

"Hush, it doesn't matter." Alan's mouth was twisted in a strange lopsided smile that made her feel even worse. "It really doesn't." He stepped back into the dark, already looking wavery and shadowy, like he'd never really been there at all.

"Wait." Sarah lurched forward and caught at his wrist. His bones were thin and sharp under her fingers, and she let go immediately.

Alan's eyes widened in surprise, but he did as she asked.

"Where do you go?" She looked at him helplessly. "Where do you disappear to?"

He smiled, slow as pouring honey, and the moon shone off his milky teeth and the white corners of his eyes.

And then he was gone.

+⁜— ⟶⟫•⟨← —⁜+

From behind Sarah came a soft sound, like the padding of a huge dog. She whipped around, half expecting to see Alan come creeping up behind her again under the moon-bright sky, trying to scare her, leave her feeling even more freaked out.

"Sometimes we need to cry," her father said. The moon shone around his shoulders, draping his hunched silhouette in a silver cloak that fell to his feet. He looked like a broken king, his hair a wild crown. Then he crouched down to hold out his hand, and the moment was gone. He was just her father, old and grizzly and tired. "Come on, let's go home. After you've slept we can talk about this properly. I didn't mean to upset you. All I want is what's right for you. And this"—he waved at the cold, open land—"none of this is right. You should be somewhere that makes you happy, somewhere safe."

Sarah didn't want to talk about any of *this* properly. All that meant was that her father would explain again how things had changed, how he couldn't cope. How he was going to send her away. Talking wasn't going to change his mind, she knew.

She let him dust the leaves from her sweater and pretended to herself that she was still just a little child. When he set off down the curly, twisty track of the Not-a-Forest, Sarah followed him home, sniffling a little every now and again. It wasn't as if she actually had anywhere else to run to, and it was cold outside. Around them the small trees leaned in and whispered the tops of their branches together. They sounded excited, passing the news between themselves like feathery trails of gossip. Sarah turned to look behind her at the little track. It was black as a child's charcoal scribble. There was no dancing flicker of fire between the slim trunks. Just empty dark, older than men and beasts.

It remembers, Alan had said. Sarah wondered if at night the trees dreamed of a time when they covered the world and the true kings were wild and wore crowns of horns and antlers.

Even if they did, she supposed it didn't matter. She was leaving her little woods behind and being sent away to people she'd never met—had believed were dead—and there was nothing left in her to feel anger or happiness or sorrow. The crying had cleaned her out like rainwater unclogging the choked-up summer leaves from a drainpipe.

The truth of it was that she didn't feel much of anything at all.

TO THE CASTLE

ONCE AGAIN, they were packing up the house. It wasn't as if this was a new thing, but before, there had been two people parceling their home into the sturdy plastic containers, wrapping the crockery and few ornaments in layers and layers of newspaper, like a backward game of pass-the-parcel, while her mother had kept a checklist on a clipboard and had marked their life away with little pencil check marks.

Sarah filled her suitcase with clothes, dog-eared paperbacks, and last of all, a thing she hadn't bothered with in years—a gift her mother had given her for her ninth birthday. She had soon stopped wearing it, because it had seemed silly. It was a small silver teddy bear on a thin necklace chain. *For my Sarahbear*, her mother had said. That was their name for her.

Even though she'd never been the kind of child who liked bears. Her two favorite stuffed toys had been a large yellow stegosaurus with purple spots and a tiny, feathery gray hedgehog that her father had brought her from a trip overseas.

Steg and Hedge were in the suitcase too, but only as somewhat grubby afterthoughts.

She picked up the necklace again. The chain swung between her fingers, the little silver bear flashing in the dim light.

Another reminder. Sarah remembered holding the bear up to her mother's necklace, one that Sarah's dad had given her, with a tiny bird on the end. It hadn't been bright and silver like the bear, but rather it looked like it had been dug out of someone's attic. Sarah had put the bear and bird together so they could talk, because it seemed rather sad that the two had to be lonely and separate all the time.

And that night her mother had brought her a small box. Inside it was her bird necklace. "At night," she said, as she unclipped Sarah's catch and lifted the necklace away in a neat shimmer of fine chain, "the two of them can be together, and talk about all the different things they've seen through the day." Her mother had closed the lid and set the little box on Sarah's night table, under the pool of light from the lamp. "And I think it's best if they stay here in the evenings, in case they have anything they need to tell you. My ears are too old to hear their voices—high-pitched, you know." And that had made perfect sense to Sarah. For years after, the box had held the two necklaces and sat on her bedside table through each night, even after she'd stopped wearing the bear.

Sarah didn't remember when the ritual had stopped, or

what had happened to the little bird. It had just been one of those things she'd grown out of and forgotten.

The bear spun gently from her fingers, alone, with no bird left to whisper to in the dark. Sarah didn't want to wear it, but she also didn't want to pack it away in one of the plastic boxes, possibly to never be seen again. So she tucked it into an envelope, dropped it on top of the neatly folded clothes, and zipped her suitcase shut.

Her father drove Sarah to her grandparents' house. He drove through the night, speeding down the empty highways, his headlights pooling cold yellow beams across the dead black tar.

They didn't talk, although her father tried a few times. Sarah just turned her face to the window and ignored him. It was to punish him, a little, but it was also because she didn't think she'd be able to say anything and not have her whole chest break open and spatter the inside of the car with all the things she was trying not to feel.

Sarah leaned her temple against the cold pane of the window. Her father wound his window down to stay awake, and night air streamed in. Sarah curled herself tighter in her blanket in the back seat, covering her face from the bite of the icy wind. She'd never liked the cold. No one in her family did.

Three times something broke the monotony of the gray-shrouded highway, as Sarah stared out her window.

First an owl swept across the road, wings silent-spread as it hunted. That was before the fog. It seemed to Sarah that the fog streamed from the owl's soft wings like downy ribbons.

Second, a hare flashed out of nowhere and died with a rattle-thump against the front grille of her father's car. It left Sarah with a sick small feeling low in her stomach, though she was too cried-out to shed any tears. After that, the fog rolled thicker across the fields to stop abruptly by the road, as if the tarmac was some kind of uncrossable river. On either side of the black strip of highway, the fog gathered like ghosts.

The third moment came just before Sarah drifted into sleep, so it could have been the beginnings of a dream. A buck with lyre-shaped horns sailed out of the bank of fog, dashed across the road, and plunged into the opposite gray mass. It was smoky under the moon, half made of mist itself.

In the dark she dreamed of her mother growing wings and darting away, out the bedroom window before Sarah could stop her. She leapt after the flying woman, but instead of growing wings herself, she fell and fell and fell.

She woke when the car came to a stop. It was still biting cold, and her cheeks were numb. Sarah uncurled from her warm cocoon of blankets and jackets and sat up blinking. The light was golden, new, and through the dust on the car window the sky was pale and pearly as the inside of a seashell.

Sometime during the night, the tarred road had given way to a smooth track of packed red sand, like a lane of beaten copper. The edges of the path were rutted by water and filled with stones, but the center line was clear. No tire tracks, no pebbles, not even the faint green wisp of a weed marred the road. On either side the grass grew pale and thin, a waist-high sea of feathery white-gold.

Sarah rubbed the sleep grit from her eyes and yawned. The car was still, parked along the side of the road. "Where are we?" she asked as she wound down the window and leaned her head out. Sleep had made her give up on the silent treatment. After all, she wasn't sure when she'd see her father again. It was so quiet here that her ears ached.

Her father was leaning against the car, drinking coffee from a thermos and smoking a cigarette. He had smoked when Sarah was a small girl; she couldn't remember exactly when he'd stopped. He seemed suddenly very young. His hair was brighter, thicker, and his skin less lined. Maybe it was the early-morning light. His eyes glinted, deep golden brown, reminding Sarah of the tigereyes in her box of semiprecious stones. "Nearer than we were," he said.

"How much farther?"

"Get out, stretch your legs a bit." He flicked ash onto the dirt road, but the wind caught the soft fluff before it hit the ground and tossed it playfully upward.

"There's no bathroom." Sarah's bladder felt full and round as a balloon filled with water. She wriggled free from the layers of blankets.

"That's what the great outdoors is for." Her father sounded almost like he was laughing, but his face was smooth and dreamy, as if he wasn't even really talking to her. Maybe he had changed his mind about this whole grandparent thing.

"Ugh. That's so gross." Nonetheless, Sarah stumbled off to find a hidden spot out in the white-gold meadow. There were no trees here, but every now and again a clump of dark-leaved shrubs huddled together in little green islands in the pale sea.

The wind chased ripples and waves through the grass tufts, and massed flocks of small birds dived in and out of the vast empty grassland.

When she came back to the car, her father had finished his coffee and cigarette, and was using the front of the car as a kitchen table, slapping pieces of ham onto white bread. He held out an uncut sandwich for her. "Breakfast," he growled.

Sarah stared at it, and then at her father's. He'd made himself a sandwich too, but instead of ham and mayonnaise, he'd added a fat layer of raw meat. It was revolting, staining the thin pieces of white bread pink. "You're not really going to eat that, are you?"

"Why?" he said. "What's wrong with it?" And he swallowed it down in two huge bites.

Sarah nibbled on the edge of her sandwich. "Okay, no more kidding around—where are we, anyway?"

"Middle of nowhere." Her father wiped his mouth with the back of his hand, then stretched so that the bones in his back popped. He turned to her and grinned. "With miles to go before we sleep."

There were tiny shreds of pink meat caught between his teeth.

+⌁— ⟶⋅⋅⟵— ⌁+

Sarah had left her nest in the back seat and changed into a pair of comfy tracksuit pants and a long-sleeved T-shirt, and was now sitting in the passenger seat, watching the world speed past.

Every now and again her father would roll down the

window for a blast of fresh cold air, and the wind would careen through the car, nipping exposed skin and tangling hair. Her father's hair seemed to have become longer and more knotted, sculpted by the wind into a wild, mussed-up mess.

Ever so slowly, the clumps of bushes grew larger, forming little knots of thorny woods. The meadows gave way to fire-blackened thickets, the thin trunks of the shrubs bedded deep in a mattress of new bracken. Here and there a lone high tree broke out above the others, like a sentinel tower. Her father's grip tightened on the steering wheel as the trees grew taller and thicker, and when Sarah glanced at his face, his mouth was clenched in a silent snarl, lips pulled back.

"Dad?" Sarah dropped her feet off the dash and sat up straighter. The trees had crowded up on either side of the road, making it harder and harder to see, but she'd caught a glimpse of something ahead. "What's that?" She pointed. There it was again, a flash of something gray.

"Ah," he said. "We're almost there." He flexed his fingers on the wheel, then raised one hand to chew absently at his thumbnail. It looked overly long and ragged, like he'd forgotten to cut his nails for months.

"Almost where?" There was no way he was taking her to her grandparents. She'd been expecting some old-age community, or even a dilapidated house in a not-so-great area. But this—they were deep in the wilds. Fear and guilt filled her. Sarah was certain that her mother had left because of her, and now she was being punished. Where was her father taking her? And why? She wasn't quite afraid of him. At least, she kept telling herself that. He was her dad, after all. He wasn't exactly lying to her, just not telling her everything. Adults were like that sometimes.

The car rounded a curve in the forest road, bumping over a thatch of dried bracken in the center, and stopped.

Ahead of them was a clearing, and in the middle of the clearing stood a castle tower.

It was a single squat turret, like a jabbing finger or a lone tooth, made of mottled stone, dribbled and spattered with lichen in yellows and reds. Furry clumps of moss clung velvety and green at the base. Ivy grew wild, so thick in some places it distorted the shape of the tower, and sprays of leaves crowned with little blue-black berries rose over the low walls around the outskirts. Tumbled boulders marked the faint outlines of rooms that had long since fallen.

Tall slitted windows cut the tower sides. Someone had hacked the ivy back from the windows, and the broken stems stuck out in ragged spikes.

"Your grandparents' house," her father said, as if it were the most natural thing in the world, and pushed open his car door.

Sarah sat frozen in place. There weren't even power lines or phone lines or anything. He was going to leave her here, out in the *middle of nowhere* in a ruin with people she'd never met. She clutched her seat belt, holding on to it desperately. Perhaps if she just never left the car, he'd be forced to drive back with her—

"Out," he said. "They're expecting you."

She swallowed, and made her fingers push the release button. There was no one waiting for them at all. Perhaps her father really had gone mad. She couldn't help but look at his hands, half expecting to see him holding an ax or something. No one would ever find her body out here.

Nothing. Of course nothing. She let herself breathe. The air tasted sweet and green, full of damp flavor. "A castle— really?" Sarah's voice sounded high and scared, though she was trying for a joke. "You never told me we were part of a royal family."

"It never seemed important," he answered. "And it's not much of a castle, either," he added. "Come on. Your grandmother will be waiting. She's old, and she likes things to happen in a timely manner."

Thoughts of a round and rosy-cheeked grandma with wispy-wool hair in a sensible bun went hurtling off into the distance. Sarah stepped out of the car and dragged her suitcase from the trunk.

It seemed heavier than ever, and Sarah wondered what would happen if she dropped her case and started crying and stamping her feet like a child, demanding they both go back to the modern and nonmagical house they'd left behind, with its empty spaces and dirty dishes. Arguing that this time they would both be better at dealing with life without Mom. She was pretty sure it would make no difference whatsoever.

Instead, with her suitcase in one hand and her day bag slung over her shoulder, Sarah turned to face her new home. On the ragged battlements a white shape hopped, sending a handful of tiny stones spattering down like hail. She squinted, shading her face with one hand, trying to get a better glimpse. It was a bird.

But not a bird *so big*. Sarah's heart gave an unexpected lurch, and the suitcase fell a few inches to slam one pointy corner into the top of her foot. She yelped and bit at her tongue, feeling her mouth spark with pain. A metal and salt taste spilled over her teeth.

"Are you all right?"

Sarah nodded. "Fine." She swallowed the taste down. The pain in her mouth and foot had turned to throbbing aches. "What kind of bird is that?"

"A raven," her father said.

"I thought they were black."

"They are."

The snowy raven stared down at her. It tilted its head, cawed once, then flew through one of the narrow windows and into the castle. It felt like an invitation.

"Do we just go in?" Sarah looked at her father uncertainly, but he was already loping past her, down a stone path. Mint and chamomile grew from the cracks in wild profusion, and her father's boots ground the flowers and leaves into perfume. Sarah took a deep breath and set off after him.

The doorway to the castle was arched, and the door itself was made of a wood so old and black and worn it looked like it had been made by giants and dwarves in some impossible faraway time. The two halves swung open as they approached, groaning on their ancient hinges.

A shadowy figure was waiting for them. A shaft of sun

pierced the dark entranceway to illuminate the tall, regal woman standing in the interior gloom. For a moment, with her back to the castle mouth and her face caught in the last rays of the pollen-dusted afternoon sun, the woman looked golden, her hair streaming behind her in thick cloud, her face stern and handsome, like in sepia photographs from long ago.

Sarah drew closer and saw the deep lines that pulled at her beauty, twisting it. Her hair was silver, not gold, and her brow was cut with a thousand frowns. Sarah's heart, which was already hanging out around the bottom of her stomach, plummeted further. Surely this angry old witch couldn't be her grandmother?

"So you've come," the woman said, looking past Sarah and at her father instead. "This is the girl?" But she still didn't look at Sarah.

Her father placed his warm hand on Sarah's back and pushed her a little closer to the woman who was supposed to be her grandmother. "This is Sarah," he said. "I said I'd bring her, and I did. Where's Father?"

"He's not well," the woman snapped.

Sarah's father didn't seem to care terribly much, but he asked, "What kind of not well?"

"You know what kind."

"Is he worse?"

Her grandmother didn't answer, just pressed her lips thinly together as if she was trying to stop a secret from inching its way out like a tiny worm.

Sarah shifted back a little, closer to her father. She didn't like this woman or the conversation. It reminded her too much of her mother's words before she left. All twisted and tangled and full of half things. Perhaps her grandmother had poisoned her grandfather. She looked like the kind of woman who would put arsenic in the soup and tenderly nurse someone to death, spoonful by spoonful. A prickling started up in the corners of Sarah's eyes. She wanted to scream at her father not to leave her here, but her words were all caught up in her throat and her tongue felt swollen to twice its size.

"I asked if he was worse," her father said, and there was a strange new deepness to his voice, like an echo under the words, like his throat was thickening all the sounds, roughening the edges. He was starting to sound like a stranger.

Sarah pushed a little sob deep down into her chest. Maybe she could escape. After her father left, she could slip away from the ruined castle and walk until she found a farm or something. People who would understand. Maybe call the police.

And then what? Where would she go? Would the authorities put her in a home filled with other children no one wanted?

Her grandmother squinted, finally peering down to get a good look at Sarah's face.

Sarah could feel her grandmother's breath against her forehead, and she realized that the old woman could hardly see. Her eyes were milky with cataracts. Maybe she *could* run away after all, if this woman was half blind.

"Hmph." Her grandmother drew back, as if Sarah was something vaguely distasteful. "She looks normal enough."

"She is," said her father. "She's normal. She's not cursed." But his voice trembled on the last word.

THE KEY OF IVORY

THE RUST-COVERED Toyota belched thick smoke into the forest clearing. The engine spat, coughed, and then with a roar, the car lurched away. Sarah's father didn't even look back at her. He raised one hand in good-bye, and that was that. He dropped it back to the steering wheel almost as soon as he'd lifted it.

Sarah and her grandmother stood silently, watching the woods darken, until the sound of the car was a distant throb. "Wastrel," said her grandmother. "Blackguard." She sniffed. "Hard to believe sometimes that he's my own true-born son."

Sarah swallowed away the snot-thick feeling of her unshed tears. "I'm Sarah," she said in a small voice.

"I know your name, girl." said her grandmother. "You will

call me Nanna. That is, after all, the kind of thing grandchildren call their beloved grandmothers."

She was nothing like a beloved grandmother. Instead Sarah was reminded of the ink drawings in her mother's battered old book of myths. Stern-faced goddesses and Fates. Terrible and strange.

Nanna drew herself straighter and held out one arm to the air. Down from the darkening skies, like a falling comet, came the white raven. It lit on her grandmother's arm and bowed, raising its beak. "And?" Nanna said.

The raven answered her in human speech. Its voice was high and sweet. "The little king is past the borderlands now." It sounded like a woman on the verge of laughing or crying.

"Hmph. Good riddance, then." Nanna twitched her arm. "The girl," she said to the raven. "He called it Sarah."

Sarah had her mouth half open, staring at the bird, trying to put together the idea that it was making words. Like a parrot. Only, no. It was talking; it was having a conversation. And it was staring at her with one ice-blue eye, head twisted to get a better look. The tiny black pupil contracted as it stared at her.

"Well met, princess," said the raven. It clacked its pickax beak. "You have your mother's look to you."

"My mother?" Sarah's heart bounced up, hope catching her by surprise. "You know her?" *I'm talking to a bird.*

"I knew her once," the white raven replied. "It has been long since last we looked upon each other. A thousand years have passed, and the forests have grown smaller. And outside the forests, your world has barely moved a decade. Or two—I can never keep track."

"Er, okay." And now it didn't seem strange to Sarah that she was having a conversation with a raven. Vaguely, she was aware that it should seem weird, but there was a dreamy quality to the dusk that made everything seem utterly reasonable, like her brain had given up trying to make sense of things and had instead just accepted defeat. *Okay, world, you win.* "I beg your pardon," she said. "but I didn't catch your name—"

Nanna laughed. "And you won't. 'Raven' will do." She twitched her wrist and the bird took flight, an ungainly flapping of large wings beating against dragging air. The raven finally soared off, leaving only a fallen white feather on the ground to mark that it had been there.

"Now," said Nanna, "I've no servants to carry your luggage about, so you'll have to do it yourself. This way." She turned into the squat castle tower, and Sarah grabbed her bags and followed her in.

It was gloomy. The stones were frozen slabs, and Sarah couldn't help but shiver. Her grandmother wore a long, thick woolen dress, and over that a coat of thick fur, dusty and moth-eaten. Dirt and black decay lay over everything. The cold seeped up from the flagstones, chilling Sarah right through her feet, all the way up her legs, so that she was shaking hard enough to rattle her teeth together.

She trod along in dejected silence, pausing only when her grandmother stopped to light sputtering candles along the walls. The candles made the air smell greasy, and they flickered and guttered in an unwelcoming way, casting leaping shadows that played out a grotesque puppet show on the stained walls. Sarah was half certain she could see actual figures choking each other, raking with their claws, could hear their screams and dying moans. She caught up quickly with Nanna, just about walking on the old woman's heels so that she wouldn't be left behind. Sarah held her bags closer.

"This will be your bedroom," Nanna said, throwing open the door of a room near the apex of the castle tower. They had taken what felt like a million stairs to get there, and Sarah was sure that her legs were going to collapse out from under her and her arms were going to fall off. She'd tried switching the suitcase from left to right, but now her arms were rubbery and limp as half-cooked spaghetti.

"It's very nice, thank you," Sarah said without really looking. All she wanted to do was curl up and sleep for a week, and hope that when she woke she would discover that all of this was just some awful nightmare.

It had to be. She lifted her head. The room was one step up from a cell. There was a single plain bed covered with dull red blankets that looked like they'd been made out of rags, and a desk with a basin and a jug. Both were yellowed enamel, the edges rough with rust.

"Good. You can clean yourself up and rest some before dinner," Nanna said. "There's an hour yet before I eat."

I, singular. Sarah cleared her throat. "Is—does my grandfather live here too?"

Nanna snorted. "In a manner of speaking." She smiled then, revealing teeth that were white and even and perfect, and Sarah wondered what she had looked like when the rest of her had matched her teeth.

There is no such thing as a perfect beauty, her mother would have told her. *Only magic.*

"Will I see him?" Sarah asked.

Nanna stared past her, eyes narrowed.

Sarah resisted the urge to look behind herself to see what the old woman was looking at. The skin on her neck began to itch. She could well believe the half-fallen castle was as thick with ghosts as it was with dust and cobwebs. Even the air smelled like fog and fallen leaves and moss.

Then Nanna blinked and shook her head. "Perhaps," she said, in a way that Sarah already knew meant no.

After her grandmother left, Sarah stood in the middle of her new bedroom and gazed numbly around her. The walls were grimed and spotted with continents of damp, and a carpet of ashy dirt covered the floor. A colony of spiders had softened the corners of the ceiling, knitted up the dust with thick skeins of silk. There was nothing caught in their webs.

Warm red light from the setting sun flowed through the narrow windows, and the lines of shadow were growing longer, creeping toward Sarah across the wooden floorboards like spilled ink. She stepped away from one particularly dark tendril and counted under her breath.

It didn't help. The tears she'd been fighting against ever since her father had told her to pack her things finally came flooding out. Sarah unzipped her suitcase, half breathless with tears, and pulled out Steg and Hedge. She didn't care if it made her seem like a frightened little kid right now. All she wanted was something familiar and cushiony to hold. With her arms wrapped tightly around the stuffed animals, crushing them against her chest, Sarah collapsed onto the small bed and sobbed until her face stung and her eyes ached and her throat felt like it had been scraped out with a fork.

When she lifted her head, the shadows were swirling all about her, and the last few red-gold gleams of the sun were just outlining her windowsill. The raven was there, cloaked in fire.

Sarah sniffed and sat up, the toys falling to the rough blanket. The raven shifted. Its claws ticked against the stone, and the sunlight slipped away, leaving the bird looking like a smear of bluish gray against the darker indigo of the sky.

"You should clean your face," the raven said in its incongruous womanly voice. "There's water in the bowl, and towels in the second drawer."

"How long were you watching me?" Sarah rubbed at her eyes and cheeks with her knuckles, then pulled one sleeve over her hand and used that to wipe her face again. "Ugh, gross." There was gunk sitting in her nose and throat.

"A few minutes only," the raven said. It sounded a little sad. "Your grandmother sent me to call you down."

"And you're her messenger or something?"

"Her eyes and ears and voice, if I need to be. I am bound to her."

"Creepy," Sarah said. She slipped from the bed and padded to the table. There were the towels, neatly folded in the second drawer as the raven had said. Ice crinkled the edges of the water in the bowl, but after the shock of the cold against her cheeks, Sarah found that wiping away the heat and shame of her tears was almost exhilarating. She glanced across at the raven, which was still watching her patiently from the windowsill. "So you're basically a spy."

The raven made no move. "Light the lamps," it said. "Unless you want to return to darkness." It spread its wings, then paused as if it was debating with itself. "By the laws of my curse, I am bound to tell her all the things I see, hear, and say within the castle," it said. "If she asks." With a crackle of feathers, it launched itself into the night.

Sarah looked at the empty place where the raven had stood and touched one thumb to her lower lip. The bird was warning her. It was a spy, true, but it sounded like it was also a slave.

It was cursed. Like everything else around her, it seemed. And as Sarah knew from her books, curses could be broken. Curses were *designed* to be broken. All it took was passing tests, she knew that. Tests of courage, of love, of wit, of faith. She frowned. How was she supposed to know what to do if she had no idea how any of this worked in the first place? There were mysteries here in this castle, in the forest, and secrets that no one was going to tell her willingly.

The thing with secrets was that they didn't want to stay secrets, Sarah mused. Someone always knew more than they should. It took the right leverage, the right pressure, and people told their hidden truths. And if that didn't work, then there was always snooping, which seemed to be the logical route in all the adventure books she loved.

Kids in stories are always going where they shouldn't and

discovering hidden treasure and evil plots and unmasking villains. And so what if that isn't real life? Sarah looked down from the castle window to the darkling forest, its whispering shadowy treetops. *Nothing about this feels like real life.*

Whatever secrets were waiting to be dug up, they had something to do with Nanna. Weirdness was gathered around her— the raven, the ruined castle all alone in the strange forest.

A new feeling crept up Sarah's back, ticking along her spine and spreading out through her shoulders. Determination. It made her feel more solid. She was going to get to the bottom of the mystery of her family. Of the curse, and what had happened to her parents.

And why.

Sarah did not get lost going down the stairs. The path she was meant to walk had been lit for her with the stubs of fat yellow-white candles in dim glass cases. The rest of the castle was dark and smelled of mouse droppings and dripping water and moldy straw, so she had no desire to stray from the lit way. Maybe tomorrow she'd have a better look in the daylight; perhaps it wouldn't seem so creepy.

She rushed down the last set of stairs, and the slap of her sneakers against the stone echoed through the hallways. Sarah's last meal had been the ham sandwich her father made for her, and a bag of chips and a soda from a gas station. She was hungry enough that she could have put up with a great deal just to fill her stomach. And the smells coming from the hall that the lights led her to were making her mouth water. Whatever

Nanna might be, she could cook—that much seemed certain. Witches could cook, Sarah thought. Well, they could brew potions, which seemed more or less the same thing.

The large hall was as gloomy as the rest of the neglected castle, but at least here the flagstones had been swept clean. Mice rustled in the cracks in the walls. At least, Sarah hoped it was nothing more unusual than mice. A few striped and ragged cats prowled the edges of the hall, their eyes stabs of pale green fire. Every now and then, one would hunch, tail whipping, then pounce on some flutter in the shadowy edges of the room.

Yes—mice. Sarah shuddered and picked her way to the large round table, where two places were set out. There were several chairs, all of them mismatched. Steaming bowls had been set before one grand chair of polished black, with thread-bare red velvet cushioning, and another, smaller one, with a seat of striped blue and gold. The material was worn, and the stuffing was sighing out of the rips. Sarah supposed this smaller one was hers.

There was no sign of her grandmother, but the raven was on the table, pacing between the dishes. "Sit," it said, and Sarah slipped into her seat.

The cushion had a tacky, squishy feel to it that made her wish she could hover above it rather than sit. "Where is she?" she whispered to the raven.

"Behind you," said Nanna. "There are no servants, or have you forgotten?"

Sarah twisted round. Her grandmother had left off her cloak of ragged fur, and she seemed somehow smaller, daintier.

Perhaps more like the way she had been as a young woman. She was carrying another covered tray, which she set down near their bowls. There was certainly a lot of food for only two people, though Sarah didn't feel inclined to point this out. Not on her very first night. She thought of her father's bloodstained teeth as he'd eaten his meat raw. Perhaps this was it—perhaps her family were secretly all monstrous carnivores and she was going to be fed platters of raw meat, lumps of cold flesh sitting in pools of sticky blood. She swallowed miserably.

Nanna took her seat and nodded at the bowl of soup in front of Sarah. "You may begin," she said.

At least soup was normal-person food. *Well, normalish.* Sarah lifted her round spoon, and gently prodded a floating piece of gristly meat. It bobbed twice, then sank. Sarah's stomach sank with it. Gingerly, she ladled herself a spoonful and sipped. It wasn't as bad as she had expected, and she plodded her way through the rest, leaving only an unidentifiable mash of small bones and soggy fat at the bottom of her bowl. There was nothing in the world that would convince her to eat that, she thought.

"Hmm," said Nanna, eyeing the remains. "Picky, are you?"

"I'm just full," Sarah lied.

"Too bad." Nanna leaned forward to open the covered dishes for the next course. There were all different kinds of meats simmering in thick juices, and a profusion of aromas curled across the table so that Sarah had to close her eyes and breathe in deeply. Meat, for sure, but cooked meat. "There's boar and hare and fawn and grouse and goose and lamb and dove." Her grandmother narrowed her eyes. "And not a bone for you, it seems. Full as you are."

The raven cawed in laughter and tipped Sarah's bowl so that the remnants spread in a gooey puddle over the pitted wood. It lunged forward, pecking out the choice pieces.

Sarah folded her hands in her lap and kept her head lowered so her grandmother would not see her face go blotchy.

Nanna ate for a long time, the only sounds the wet sucking of her lips and the brittle clack of bones returned to the plate. Finally, it seemed Nanna had consumed all she could. She pushed her plate a little away from herself and leaned back in her chair.

Sarah looked up to see her scrape all the leftovers into the largest pot and cover it up. "Come along," Nanna said as she stood. She lifted the full pot and cradled it with both arms. "I think it's time you met your grandfather, after all."

Sarah's heart lurched. What was she to expect—an old, bedridden man? An ax-wielding maniac locked up for his own good? The soup sloshed about inside her, making her feel queasy, and Sarah pressed her thumbs hard against her legs, focusing on that until the feeling passed. She wished she were out of this place. Anywhere, it didn't matter. As long as it was a million miles away from here and now.

The white raven launched itself up to perch on Nanna's shoulder and rubbed its beak against her earlobe. "Come along, along, a long way to come," it chattered. Sarah was now convinced that it was insane. Just like Nanna. And herself, probably.

The raven and the old woman led the way out of the

castle, into the circle of empty night that surrounded the stone building. Perhaps her grandmother was going to lead her off into the forest and just . . . leave her there, to be eaten by whatever monsters lurked.

Instead she walked a well-worn track that curved behind the main body of the turret. In the lee of the building was a rough shack, in the same state of disrepair as the rest of the castle, its rotted straw roof ragged and dripping black mold. The smell of loam and earthy decay was everywhere, but over it was another, stronger smell, rank and musky.

Sarah edged back, the smell assaulting her nostrils. There was something in it that reminded her of one of the houses they'd once moved into. There'd been a playhouse at the back of the garden, but Sarah's initial excitement had come crashing down when they'd found feral cats had been using it to live in. There was a sour ammonia smell of pee that no amount of scrubbing had been able to lift. That smell was here too. Only a thousand times worse, mixed with the sweet-gross smell of spoiled meat and decay.

Nanna bent to push open the door to the hovel with her elbow. "This way, girl," she muttered as she looked back, catching Sarah with a wicked gleam of her eye. Reluctantly, Sarah followed her into the darkness. The floor of the shack was thick clay mud, and it sucked at Sarah's shoes, like hands unwilling to release a captive. The stink was stronger inside. As Sarah's eyes adjusted to the darkness, she could finally see where the stench was coming from. Most of the shack was taken up with a simple iron cage. The metal was black and wet-looking under the thin moonlight that slanted through the broken roof.

Inside the cage was a beast. At first Sarah thought it was a bear, with its head lowered between great hunched shoulders, but then it moved and it was clear that this was no creature she'd ever seen in any book, or on television or at the zoo. There was the essence of bear, yes, but also of wolf, of lion. It was a king beast, great and gray, with coarse fur like matted wires, teeth long as her fingers, eyes like lost planets.

The beast turned in its cage as Nanna set the pot down and fished out a small, ornate key on a slender chain around her neck. The key seemed a ridiculous thing, pale as finger-nail parings, but as Nanna held it she whispered, and the key grew larger, sharper, wicked-looking.

Sarah rubbed at her eyes, and then firmly decided to put it down to a trick of the light.

Nanna bowed down to unlock the small door, shoved the pot in, then slammed the door shut as quickly as she could. All through the shack the sound crashed, making the walls shiver, and the wet timbers dropped flakes of gunky dirt down on their heads.

The beast raised one huge clawed paw—more like a hand—and batted at the pot, spilling the meat and bones into the mildewed straw that covered the floor of its cage.

From the cage came the most awful sounds. A crunching, splintering cacophony. A gnawing and grinding and sucking. Sarah hugged herself tightly and breathed out through her nose, too scared now to move. *It's not real. None of this is real. Wake up. Wake up.* She pinched her arm through the thick knit of her sweater, twisting hard enough to know that she'd be bruised in the morning, but nothing about the scene changed.

Nanna said nothing while the beast fed. When it was done, she hooked the pot out and locked the cage again. Another whisper, and the key shrank in her hands till it was no bigger than the first joint of Sarah's smallest finger. She tucked it into her dress again. "There," she said to Sarah. "Now you've met him, the one who carries the curse and passed it on to my son. The man who has tied me to this place, and tied your father, and now you in your turn."

Sarah's arms felt limp, the bones turned to custard. They fell to her side with all the strength sucked out of them. Her legs felt just as useless. She needed to get out of there. With an immense deep breath and a force of will she wasn't sure how she was able to muster, Sarah staggered backward, away from the thing in the cage. Away from the woman who kept him there.

Was this what her mother and father had meant when they'd whispered about curses? It had to be. It *couldn't* be. This was what her mother had run away from, and it was in Sarah's family, in their blood. *The curse.* The curse that hadn't touched her, or so her father had said.

She turned and scrabbled at the door, flinging it open so she could run out into the cold air, with the cackle of Nanna's laughter and the echoing raven caws following her.

7

IN CAPTIVITY

MORNING CAME filtering into Sarah's room, creeping in on fog-feet. She woke into a silence that was thick and muffled, as if the whole castle was enveloped in cloud. Even the light was hazy. She stretched, working out the cramps in her legs and back.

Last night she'd run back here because there was nowhere else to go. It all seemed distant and broken, like the last traces of a nightmare already slipping away. Sarah was still wearing the jeans and sweatshirt she'd changed into before dinner. She had both arms wrapped around her stuffed animals, and their faces were sodden with her tears.

She looked down. Her muddy sneakers were laced on her feet, and she'd left smears of red mud all over the blanket.

"Ugh," Sarah said, shoving her companions to one side. Her eyes were puffy and tight. Not surprising, since she'd sobbed herself to sleep. "You are making an awful habit of bursting into tears over everything," she told herself sternly, but it didn't make her feel any better. She made herself uncurl and hobble over to the bowl of icy water. The candles had burned out in the night, leaving smears of greasy dark wax in the hollows of the glass lanterns. Someone had come and left a bundle of fresh white candles on her desk. They were tied together with rough brown cord. *Nanna.*

There were no servants, her grandmother had told her. And that could only mean that her grandmother had been in here last night while Sarah slept. A shudder traveled down her body. Just the thought that the creepy old woman had been sneaking through her room while she was dreaming was horrifying enough, but there was that . . . thing.

That thing—the beast—in the cage. It couldn't really be her grandfather. There was no curse, no magic. In the light of day, such a thing seemed impossible. The raven was trained to talk. Or there were speakers and microphones set up all around the castle. Even here in her room.

The realization was dizzying. She was completely alone with a madwoman. And her father was the one who had left her there. Sarah cupped water in her palms and splashed it on her face. The cold made her gasp, but it was a good, fierce kind of shock, like being slapped back to reality.

If there were microphones and speakers in the room, there could be cameras too. There would be electricity—despite the candle lanterns. It was like she was on a deranged film set.

And whatever Nanna said about how she had no servants, it was a lie. There were people helping her grandmother—people who set all this up, made the food. Someone had to have designed the beast costume and worn it. Or maybe it was some kind of robotics . . .

Why would anyone do all this just to terrify her? Sarah rubbed her hands over her face. *How is this not more insane than believing in magic?*

There were two truths, but they couldn't both be true at the same time.

"I don't know what I believe," Sarah said fiercely into her hands. *I don't know what's real.*

She lowered her hands and held on to the desk, almost as if it was the only thing that could stop her spinning off the face of the earth. *They're both impossible. Or improbable.*

Not for the first time in her life, Sarah wished that her parents had agreed to buy her a cell phone. It had always felt to her like she was the only one in her class who didn't have one, but her parents had been adamant that they hadn't needed cell phones when they were children and she would survive just fine without one. *Hah. So much for that.*

Sarah looked around the room. *Okay. No phone. And nowhere to charge it even if I did have one. And probably no reception anyway.* How had people gotten hold of each other in the dark ages of her parents' childhood—letters?

Sarah brightened a little. They couldn't be completely cut off here. Someone had to make deliveries—there was a road, after all. She would find a way to get help. Quickly, she stripped down and washed herself with cold water and changed into clean clothes. Today she would explore what she could, and find out what was real and what wasn't. She didn't care too much about the castle; that was her grandmother's realm, and there was no escaping it. No, there were other paths to follow.

There are ways to get free, Sarah thought. *There have to be. And I'll find them no matter what. But first, I think Nanna owes me some answers.*

She dressed warmly against the constant chill and, almost as an afterthought, slipped the little silver teddy pendant over her head. It wasn't because her mother had given it to her, she told herself, but just that it was something real, and it came from a time when things had been mostly normal. It settled under her T-shirt, cold against her skin, then quickly warmed. Sarah cupped her hand over it and breathed deeply.

Out here, far away from any cities, everything smelled more strongly. It was like scent had become as solid and undeniable as sight. Sarah could smell bacon, the greasy sulfur of eggs, the cold tang of the mud below, the green, dark spice of the forest. She could smell the clouds, the rainy potential of them waiting to break open. Sarah closed her eyes. She could even smell the stones, their flint and the weight of their years. Weird.

Maybe it was because there was nothing else to distract her from really concentrating. She dropped her hand away from the little hidden bear and went down to the kitchen, ready to face the woman who called herself her grandmother, and demand to know exactly what was going on.

Sarah raced down the echoing stairs, glanced into the hall where she'd eaten last night, and saw no one. The table had been cleared. She paused. Faintly, from below, came the clanking of pots and dishes.

That had to be from the other people in the castle. The ones who were helping her grandmother in this ridiculous deception. The bird had been a good trick, though—it had seemed so real. Last night, tired and scared, she'd truly believed in curses and magic and all kinds of childish nonsense.

"Raven?" Sarah called out, but the large room stayed quiet. She shook her head. The bird was just a well-trained pet. Maybe it was microchipped so that her grandmother could trace it wherever it went, or—

Stop it, Sarah thought. *Assume nothing. Trust nothing.* She stepped away from the open door. If all of this was a huge setup, if none of it was *really* real, then the first thing she wanted to do was go see the beast. Whatever it was—living creature or a mess of wires and metal and fur. All the truth would be revealed if she could just see for herself.

◦⟶•⟵◦

The air outside was clammy with the promise of rain. If anyone had noticed Sarah slipping out the wide castle door, they weren't doing anything about it. It was easy enough to see the path she'd taken last night. The mud had dried a little in ridges and waves, but the footprints she and Nanna had left were clear enough. The path was worn deep through the grass—it had been there a long time. She picked her way along the track, and the dew-heavy grasses wiped their tears against her jeans, soaking the cuffs and her sneakers, until each step sounded with a soggy squelch. Tiny spiderwebs hung with diamonds glittered in the pale sunshine, looking like fairy castles tucked away in the tanglehead grass.

She followed the track around to the back of the castle, and as she did, a faint mist slithered out from the forest and began to follow her. It grew thicker with every step she took, curling around her feet and blanketing away the spider-castles. Above, the sun grew dimmer, peering through a lacework of dark clouds.

Now the path was swallowed up, and hulking dark shapes loomed out of the fog. Sarah approached them with trepidation, only to find they were merely the rusting remains of ancient farm machinery. She hadn't seen these last night; it had been too dark, the only light coming from her grandmother's lamp. She slowed down, peering at each abandoned husk.

There was something that had once been a car, but any hope that it would ever run was quickly flattened as she drew nearer. It rested on its axles, and it was nothing more than scrap. One door hung half off its hinges, and inside the seats were covered with straw; small weeds grew through the rusted floor. Sarah stuck her head in an open window. A pair of sleepy hens clucked at her from the back, their amber eyes conveying annoyed boredom.

"Sorry," Sarah said, and pulled back from the car door. The rust left wet red smears on her palms. This wasn't why she was here—looking for hens and cars that would never run. She peered over the roof, and there it was: the small shed.

It looked bigger in the daylight, the mist dragging at its walls, moisture sliding down from the straw eaves to plop steadily in the mud. The top of the straw roof was black, and a few pale stems jutted out from underneath. Sarah stepped under the eaves and tugged at one straw. It pulled out easily, like a loose tooth. Sarah dropped the piece of straw into the mud at her feet and, with a deep breath, examined the door.

It was a stable door with both halves held closed by old iron bolts. Like everything else here, the metal was rough and etched with rust. Stains from the eroding metal wept redly down the scarred paint. Someone had once painted the door a bright and cheery blue, the color of a new summer sky, but now the paint was cracked, and long strips had peeled away to reveal wood that was slowly blackening. It looked pulpy and rotten. If there really was a beast kept in here, the door would do nothing to stop it from breaking free, if ever her grandmother forgot to lock the cage.

There's no beast . . .

Sarah glanced behind her to where the ivy-covered castle walls poked up through the low fog, but the castle windows were too narrow for her to see anything. Certainly, it didn't *look* like anyone was watching her. She shook her head and tiptoed to the door. The bolts were stiff, and she wrestled a little with them before they scraped back.

Okay, the moment of truth. She pulled.

The reek slapped her—meaty, musky, wild. The stink of wet dog multiplied a thousand times; cat urine and the too-sweet smell of rotting things. In the daylight it seemed slightly more bearable. Even so, it was a rank and ugly smell.

"Hello?" Sarah said into the interior of the hut. The windows let in no light, and Sarah guessed that they'd been boarded up, or were too filthy to do any good. The only light came from the doorway, and she was blocking most of it. She stood on the threshold, not really wanting to set foot inside that room even if it would solve one mystery.

Nothing answered her.

Animatronics. It had to have been. Or some kind of puppet. She cleared her throat and spoke louder. "If there's anyone in here—"

Something shifted in the gloom, and the darkness that filled the cottage moved.

"You can come out now . . ." Sarah's voice faltered.

"Girl." The voice was gruff, and so thick that Sarah almost wasn't sure it had actually said a word, or if her overactive imagination had just turned some animal growl into one.

"Oh dear," Sarah said, and fervently wished that she had stayed back in her room and pretended to be a good granddaughter and hadn't even had the slightest thought of exploring or trying to solve any mysteries. She should have sat in her room and read her books, or played make-believe with Steg and Hedge, even if that seemed silly and childish and not real at all.

Right now silly and childish and not real sounded very appealing. "Um." Sarah edged back, ready to slam the stable door shut and bolt it up again.

"Wait," said the darkness. It moved again, and Sarah could see the outlines of the iron cage, and the hulking shape trapped inside it. "Come closer."

"Um," said Sarah again. "I can hear you perfectly well from here, actually, if that's all right."

"You—" The voice coughed, growled, then it sounded

like whoever was talking spat a thick wad of *something* onto the ground, where it landed with a raw splat.

Sarah closed her eyes and grimaced.

"You were here last night," the beast tried again. "With Inga."

"Nanna," Sarah whispered in answer. "With Nanna."

"Ah," said the beast. "So you're truly our grandchild, then."

Not a beast. A man in a costume. A prank. A stupid game to scare me. Sarah mustered up her courage with a deep breath and stepped farther into the crumbling shed. "I'm not afraid of you," she said. "I've worked it all out. It's tricks and stuff."

"What is?"

"This. You." Sarah waved in the direction of the iron bars and the vast furry shape behind them. "I don't know why, and it's not funny, but I know that none of this is real." *I know.*

"Inga brought you to me last night, that you would see and understand." Two lights like lamps shone suddenly in the gloom, and Sarah realized that until now the beast's head had been turned away from her. "If I am just a trick, then step closer."

"Look, I'm not totally stupid," Sarah said. "I don't need to get any closer to you, really."

"But how then can I make you believe?" The beast moved again, turning to face her completely. It was easier to see him now—scarily easy. "Closer."

Sarah shifted forward despite her fear, and something cracked under her foot. She looked down. In the filthy scattered straw she could make out other pale shapes: long thin bones and tiny skulls. Her breathing hitched.

This was a lot of effort to go to just to get the atmosphere right.

Sarah's face grew numb and cold, and her breathing went ragged. *No. Please, no.* But she kept walking.

Finally, she was close enough to the iron bars to be able to reach a hand through to touch the hunched thing inside it, if she'd wanted to. Which she didn't. Except she did, just a little bit. *Curiosity killed the cat.*

"Look at me."

Sarah raised her head and stared into the huge amber eyes of the beast. They were round and golden, flecked with starry silver points and motes of drifting darkness. The slitted pupils seemed to throb wider in the center of this golden haze of sun rays. Not fake eyes. Not glass. His breath, meaty and stinking, puffed against her face.

Now she saw his ears trembling, the fine hairs tufting dark. Behind them, bursting from the matted coat, were two coiled ram's horns.

He smiled, pulling back his ragged lips to show long yellow teeth, curving to dull points. He could crush her head in his mouth. Saliva gathered in frothy loops from those soft, rippled black gums, and dripped to the floor.

"No," said Sarah. She felt rooted in place, unable to step away from the thing before her, but still not wanting to believe it.

"Touch me, and know the truth," said her grandfather. His deep growl was hypnotic, smoothing away her fear.

Her hand lifted, and she snaked her wrist between the bars

to settle her fingers above the cold black nose. The beast—her grandfather—was warm, the fur rough under the pads of her fingers.

He huffed and pushed his nose against her hand, and Sarah stood, stroking the vast muzzle of the thing in the cage. Beast. Grandparent. She couldn't be sure, but that didn't matter.

There was no denying the reality of the creature's existence. And the reality of his circumstances. He was hunched into a cage too small for him to walk in, his fur was matted with filth and his own droppings, spoiled food covered the floor of his prison.

The beast sighed and closed his eyes, shifting his head so that Sarah could reach up and scratch behind his ears, her nails pulling away the tangles from the base of the nearest horn. Metal clanked, and when Sarah crouched down a little, she could see the manacles that had worn away the fur above his massive paws, had chewed the bare skin raw.

"Oh, Grandfather," she whispered.

"What are you doing here?" A woman's voice shrieked from behind her, and Sarah whipped around to see a small white shape in the doorway.

The raven hopped inside. "You may not be here without your grandmother. Step back!"

Sarah hesitated, and the raven cried again, panic making its beautiful high voice sharp and angry. "Back! Back!" It flapped its wings. "There is no trusting the beast!"

This brought a pained growl from the beast, and Sarah pulled her hand back out of the bars and stumbled away. The beast was looking at her again, golden eyes so bright that it made the rest of his shape nothing more than a dark shadow in darker shadows.

"I'm—I'm sorry," she said, not knowing what she was apologizing for, and ran out into the sunlight.

The mist had lifted and the forest was a shimmering peridot wall around the castle clearing. The bright sky was washed blue. Everything was clear, almost glowing in the sunlight. The little nets of spiderwebs had dried away, and the clumps of grass stood high and green, their ribbon-twisted blades dancing in the breeze.

The door to the shack swung closed of its own accord, the bolts screeching back into place.

Sarah shuddered. There was no denying now what she had seen. She swung around to where the raven was standing on the roof of the ruined car, much to the dismay of the hens inside, who were clucking furiously. Sarah lunged forward and caught the raven by surprise, closing her hands around its feathery body. The bird struggled, cawing in indignation, but Sarah held fast, pinning its wings flat to its sides.

"What," Sarah said, very slowly, "is going on? Tell me now and tell me everything." She slid one hand higher, tightening her grip, as she felt the bird's heart thrumming under the joint of her thumb. "Or I will wring this scrawny neck of yours, you see if I don't."

YOU CAN'T LIFT CURSES
WITH KISSES

AN ARCTIC WIND shivered through the trees, causing their great shaggy heads to bow closer as if they wanted to hear what the raven would say. The bird went limp and unresisting. "You wouldn't really?"

"I don't *think* I would," Sarah said, then decided that didn't quite sound menacing enough. "But I've never really been in a situation where I've wanted to." She paused and glared at the raven. "I may be getting there."

"Let me go, and I swear I'll tell you all you need to know."

"And who decides what that is—you? No." Sarah shook her head. "Everything."

"On my honor," the raven said. "Everything."

"Okay." Sarah lifted one hand away, and the raven hopped

free, to land some distance from her on the far side of the car. It stared at her from its perch on the roof. "I'm waiting," said Sarah. "Or do birds not have honor?"

"We're not safe here," said the raven. It looked up at the bulk of the castle, which was throwing a misshapen shadow across the clearing. "Follow." It threw itself up into the air and flapped toward the forest.

The trees were crowded together, their trunks too close, knitting a solid fence around the castle and hemming her in. Sarah gritted her teeth. *What is it about the forest that's so terrifying, anyway? It's not like the trees are any creepier than the castle.*

Maybe because it was not a little piece of forest, but a great one. Sarah wondered what this kind of primordial forest would remember.

A tall figure flickered in the arboreal dark, a shape flitting between the trunks. Sarah opened her mouth, certain she'd seen a face staring out at her under a cap of russet hair, but then the thing in the forest moved again, and whether it was the stretching shadows or the close-packed trunks that had confused her, the shape looked now more like an antlered buck, pausing to watch the human who stood at the forest's border.

It was just a deer. She didn't linger too long on how for one moment she'd thought the deer was a lanky stripling named Alan, and she'd been about to call his name out in greeting. Instead, she set off in the direction the raven had flown.

The edge of the forest was cool, the trunks mossy and green, some of them completely choked with ivy. Faint beams of light filtered through the canopy, dappling the leaf litter. Small mouselike birds fluttered among the upper branches, and a squirrel chittered at her from one high branch, then ran up into the canopy. Sarah took a few more hesitant steps into the gloom and almost walked into a low-strung spiderweb.

She ducked, and the webs shivered as her hair caught on the thick strands. There wasn't just one. Several vast webs stretched between the branches, each holding a yellow and black spider like a bright sweet at its center. The spiders were thumb-sized, their webs catching the weak light and glinting golden. They lined the narrow little animal paths like the walls of an ethereal labyrinth.

"Raven?" Sarah called nervously.

"This way." A moon-white shape sailed overhead and landed with a thump on a branch wreathed with greenish old-man's beard. The raven edged along the tapering walkway and leapt to another, always staying ahead, leading Sarah through the maze of trees and golden webs, deeper into the forest.

"Where are we going?" The trees grew far enough apart from each other to allow easy walking, but some of the branches were low, and Sarah had to hold them aside so she could follow. The leaves were prickle-edged and bit into her freezing hands. She'd never seen trees like this before, but that didn't mean much—she'd never really been botanically inclined. Some of the thinner twigs snapped as she passed, and a spicy, bitter scent followed her.

It was getting colder; her breath puffed up in little clouds of smoke.

"To the center," said the raven. "Or as close to the Within as we can get."

"What's the Within?" A branch slapped Sarah across the

cheek, the spiky leaves catching at her eye. "Ow, wait." She wiped the sting away and rubbed her cheek. It was definitely getting colder. There was frost trimming diamond skins on the leaves and twigs.

"Where the witches used to live." The raven stopped. From a distance came a cold burble of running water. "Your grand-mother cannot go into the Within, so the land around it is safe from her."

"Witches." Sarah hugged herself and rubbed her arms with her palms, trying to warm up. She stamped her feet and the ice on the ground crushed softly beneath her shoes. "I don't want to go anywhere near witches." If there were cursed beasts who crushed skulls between their teeth just below the castle, then she didn't want to consider what witches deep in a forest were like. Like they were in the old stories, probably—child-eaters and poisoners.

"You've nothing to fear from the witches now," the raven said. "There aren't any left, just beast-boys and creatures that used to belong to the Within."

"I don't like this," Sarah whispered. They were now so deep into the forest that not even the faintest sunbeam could squeeze its way down. There were patches of ice crisping the ground, and icicles dripped from the shadowy spokes of the trees.

"Here we are," said the raven, and Sarah followed the flash of its white feathers to an open spot. The sun was cold and far away, but at least there *was* sun. It sparked off patches of fallen snow, and off the steel-gray waters of a turbulent river. That was where the sound of water had been coming from. It looked fast. The edges were cloudy with ice, but the middle was a deep black-green that made Sarah shiver right down to her soles. Under the surface the stones rolled, crashing against one another.

"You may speak with safety. Your grandmother will hear nothing said here, even to me. Her reign extends only so far."

Sarah narrowed her eyes. "How can I believe that?"

"You can't." The raven shuddered, half-opening its wings. "You have only faith."

"Um, yeah. I don't think I have faith in anything here, especially you." Sarah rubbed her nose. It was reassuring to find it still there, as it had now gone completely numb from the cold. And her cheeks were starting to burn. "But if it's a choice between you and Nanna, I guess . . ." Sarah dropped her hand and sighed. "Okay, the truth then—what's going on? And what's the curse everyone's talking about?"

The raven dipped the front of its body in a little bow, and began. "Your grandfather was once a beautiful prince, and like many beautiful people, vain and selfish. He had the pick of women of the woods and the castle—all kinds, ones with power and ones without, the pretty and the plain and the in-between. And like all foolish, vain people, instead of choosing a woman he loved, he chose a prize to look pretty on his arm.

"I would like to say that the bride he picked was as foolish and vain as he was, but perhaps she was just young. At any rate, she was not rich in magic, and even poorer in wisdom, but she had looks and charm and she saw the prince and wanted him. Many beautiful people are interested only in mirrors."

"They both sound . . . wonderful." But then again, who

knew if the raven was really telling the truth. "So what happened?"

The raven puffed up. "The bride was an orphan who had been taken in by foster parents, and their true daughter was a powerful witch. And this witch-maiden could see that the prince and his chosen were not truly in love with each other, but were so captured by each other's beauty that they could not see those who *did* love them, and treated those people with blind cruelty. So on the evening of their wedding, she set a curse on her foster sister and her prince."

"Nice." Sarah rolled her eyes.

"It was only fair, to show them both the depths of their vanity. The witch-maiden cursed the prince to change into a beast the moment he truly fell in love with his bride."

"That seems odd. And not exactly fair."

"You would be surprised how often people fall in love with their own reflections," the raven snapped. "And he would be doomed to stay a beast until she loved him equally in return."

Sarah was quiet for a while. "Is she that hateful—Nanna? Did she realize that he'd fallen in love with her, and then instead of feeling anything, she just kept him in a cage forever?"

"No." The raven almost looked like it was smiling. "By the terms of the curse, she must stay with him or die."

"Nanna will die if she leaves my grandfather, even though he's a beast? Why would anyone be so cruel?" Sarah hugged herself. Things were looking darker, and she wasn't certain she wanted to hear how the curses all twisted together.

The raven cawed, a sound of malicious triumph. "Maybe

she deserved it. The witch-maiden was smart, she knew how these things go. The girl—the beautiful, empty-headed girl—would never leave her beast no matter how loathsome she found him, because she couldn't. She was cursed to stay by his side until death."

"I don't get it. So if Nanna has to stay with him, where do you come in?"

The raven puffed up its feathers, so it resembled a rather startled snowball. "That has nothing to do with this story," it said. "And I don't have to tell you."

Sarah rubbed her freezing hands against her face, and blew into them. She was starting to suspect the raven was mad—well, madder than previously thought. "I still don't see why he can't just make her fall in love with him so he stops being a beast and everything ends happily ever after." Sarah shrugged. "Isn't that how these things usually go?"

The sound of the river grew louder as it clawed at its banks. Snow slid from a weighted branch and dropped with a thump that shook ice-sharp rain from the trees. The raven regarded Sarah with solemn patience.

"You can't make someone fall in love with you," the raven said when it finally spoke. "I should know. And that is where the storytellers write their own sugary versions of the truth. A pack of lies until they reach 'The End.' But no story ever comes to an end, at least not one so neat. There are voices silenced, characters erased at the storyteller's whim." The bird clacked its beak. "They do not tell you what happens when the children have eaten their way through the witch's treasures and face another starveling winter, when the glass slipper no longer fits the crone's swollen foot, when the beauty doesn't fall in love with her beastly prince."

Sarah felt deeply uncomfortable. "I hate this story," she said. The raven was lying to Sarah, she knew it—taunting her for amusement. Nothing it said could be trusted.

The raven cawed in laughter. "I told you the witch-maiden was clever. She knew that even if Inga did ever fall in love and the curse turned the monster back into a man, she would always know that her prince might go back to being a beast if she fell out of love again. It made it harder for her to fall in love in the first place. No love is endless."

"That's not true!"

"Oho! Is that what you think? Why did your mother fly?" The raven stared, head cocked. "People fall out of love slower than they fall in, to be sure, but there's the story no one wants to tell. It's dull. Boring. The good ones don't always win. Nothing lasts forever."

A ragged wind had picked up and was winding its way through the branches, rolling a blanket of clouds over the distant sun.

"I don't believe you." Sarah shook her head. "I won't believe you."

It became colder—impossibly colder—and Sarah, who had already pulled her sleeves over her aching fingers, crossed her arms and tucked her curled-up hands into her armpits. The warmth there wasn't enough, her fingers chilled right through her sweater to the tender skin of her underarms. She was shivering now so hard that her teeth were rattling in her jaw like dice in a cup. "So," she said, through the ivory chatter of her teeth, "my grandmother never loved my grandfather, and he had to stay a beast? Is that what you're saying? The curse could never really be broken?"

"There are curses layered on curses in your family, secrets so deep and dark that your parents and grandparents refused to face them," said the raven. "Your grandfather became beast and burden, for your grandmother had bound herself to him as tight as any bride could. She made him promises on that wedding day, promises she could not keep—that she would love him always, that they would only ever be happy."

Sarah swallowed hard. The things that the raven was telling her couldn't be true. They were too ugly. "So she keeps him in a cage and feeds him leftovers—why not set him free and go? Surely they'd both be happier."

"I told you, she cannot. She is as cursed as he is. She gave her word, and the witch-maiden made sure that it was a marriage bond she could never break." The raven watched Sarah with one pale blue eye, its head twisted so that it could stare balefully at her. "It is a curse that binds your family; it wraps them up tighter than rope and chains, for it is a curse of their own making. The witch-maiden cast it not only on those two foolish, vapid people, but on all their line, for all eternity."

"Oh," Sarah said, and sniffed. The cold was making her nose run. "Is my father cursed then, too?"

The raven's eyes gleamed. "What do you think?"

Yes, Sarah thought, before she could try to convince herself otherwise. Her mother had left him, not bound by any curses to stay when her own love failed, and now her father was turning. How long before he too was an animal, like his father? Was that why he'd sent her away, so she wouldn't have to see his fall? "That's not fair," she whispered. "He's only half a beast."

"And you only a quarter," snapped the raven. "Curses have no care for the thinness of your blood."

"I'm—I'm not cursed, they said."

"And you believe them." Sarah could hear the laughter in its voice, cold and brutal. A talking raven, another beast.

Sarah hugged herself tighter. "I don't care if you say you're not part of this story. You are, or you wouldn't be here. Tell me the truth."

"Oh, me," said the raven, and bobbed its head as if it were curtsying before a queen. "We're all cursed here." And it would say no more. Eventually, Sarah supposed it couldn't, and that was that.

The darkening sky was pressing down, the river running faster beneath its icy shards, churning the snow at its edges to slush. "We'd best be back," the raven said. "You may come here again if you need a moment away from her, but on no account try to cross the river. Its price is too high, and the Within is not a place for you."

"Why's that?" Sarah asked as she scrambled back to the little track that ran between the black trunks. Rain had begun to hiss against the uppermost leaves, and a few drops were plopping down through the thick canopy.

"The Within is the heart of all curses. There the witch

wove the spells that turned your family, that bound them in their strange skins. It is a place thick with ancient power, where the witch-maiden made her home, the root of her magic—why would you go there and tempt the curse to wake inside you?"

Another branch slapped forward into Sarah's face, grazing her chin, cutting a thin line across her lower lip. She licked, tasted the blood. Sarah was beginning to think that the forest had a mind of its own, that it wanted her to stay. The going back was harder than the leaving had been. But perhaps there was a good reason for that. Perhaps the forest was trying to tell her something. "Things that make curses, they can unmake them too," she said harshly. "If the Within is where the witch's power comes from, and the witch is gone, maybe it just needs someone else to use that power."

"Oho," said the raven, and flew far ahead, till it was nothing more than a white star in the green and black heavens of the forest dark. Sarah could hear the soft caw in the distance as she battled her way through the close-growing trees.

Oho, oho.

+⫯— ⟶·⟵ —⫯+

The rain was a steady downpour by the time Sarah reached the castle. She raced across the clearing, hopping over the clumps of tangled blackjack weeds and wiry grass. Even though the rain pelted down, at least it was warmer here. Sarah ran under the stone archway and stopped before the great wooden door, her hair dark and dripping. The door was locked against her, or it was too heavy for her to budge.

She settled on rapping her knuckles against the black wood, so hard that the bones felt shattered under her skin.

Finally the doors groaned and swung outward, so that Sarah had to jump back a little. Nanna stood on the other side, stern-faced and gray like a standing stone. But also dry.

"Um, I was exploring," Sarah said, even though Nanna hadn't asked. "And I got a little lost."

"Hmph," said Nanna, but she stepped aside. "Come in out of the wet, fool girl. You've missed breakfast," she added as the doors closed behind Sarah, through their own power, it seemed.

Magic.

"Sorry," Sarah mumbled. She shivered in her damp clothes.

Her grandmother snorted and snapped her fingers in impatience.

Heat flickered over Sarah's skin, snake-fast, and as soon as it was gone, Sarah's clothes were dry. Bone dry, and her hair, which had been hanging in dripping tails, was warm and soft.

Magic.

There was no way she could carry on denying it. And if it was all true, then the raven wasn't lying either. *Cursed.* She thought of the beast outside in the shed, and how the water must be pouring through the holes in the roof, how the beast—how Grandfather—would be lying in mud, would be cold and damp and with no chance of respite. "Um," Sarah said again.

Her grandmother was striding along the corridors and hallways, and down a flight of unlit stairs. The castle was already a gloomy place, but with the storm growling and spitting overhead, it was even darker and gloomier. Sarah hurried to catch up.

They came to a vast underground kitchen. Here, at least, were warmth and lanterns and huge iron ranges with pots of gleaming copper. A spoon swirled lazily by itself in one bubbling stewpot, and the aroma of beef and vegetables and garlic hung heavy. Nanna pointed to a covered plate on the huge kitchen table. "Your eggs will be cold, but that's hardly my problem. Sit. Eat."

Nanna was right, the eggs were cold, and so were the bacon and the toast, but they were still there. Another snap of her fingers, and steam rose from the plate. "And that's more than you deserve," she said. "Now. What is it you wanted?"

At least Nanna hadn't decided to start starving her, Sarah mused. The way things had been going for her, that was almost a relief. "It's about Grandfather," Sarah said, and then quickly took a bite of toast to give herself something to do. And because she was hungry. It turned out that fighting your way through a snowy forest before breakfast did severe things to the appetite.

"What about him?" Nanna asked flatly. She'd crossed her arms and was staring narrowly at Sarah. Behind her the pots bubbled to themselves, the spoons stirred, the smells wafted.

Sarah swallowed her toast. "Well . . . it's . . . he's probably cold and wet where he is now, right?"

"And what would you have me do—bring him in here to keep him dry?" Nanna sniffed. "I think not. He's a beast now, and that's all there is to it. Beasts have hungers. They can't be trusted."

"And beastkeepers?" asked Sarah.

Nanna said nothing. Instead she looked at the table very hard, as if by staring at it long enough she could turn it into something else, or make it prance about on its four legs. Possibly she could. "Eat your food," she said finally. "There are chores that need doing."

Sarah pushed a crispy piece of bacon through the remains of her eggs. "Nanna?"

"What is it now?"

"What happens if you leave here?"

Instead of answering, her grandmother stared at her for a full minute, then, grim-faced, she got up and swept from the room, her skirt trailing like the broken wings of a bird.

WE MUST BE ENEMIES

IT TURNED OUT that Nanna's idea of chores all seemed to be ones that kept Sarah outdoors. Whatever it was that kept the castle running, or fueled Nanna's magic, perhaps it didn't extend to the grounds.

That was fine by Sarah; the castle gave her the creeps. Every moment she was inside its walls she felt as if she were being slowly crushed in a damp stone fist. Even if the sunlight outside was thin and not very warm, it was better than the choking dust and mold inside. And it helped to not be around her grandmother.

Nanna set Sarah to weeding an area that had once been a vegetable garden. There were still some straggling, yellowed cabbages among the weeds, and a few shriveled beans here and there, but mostly the garden had been left to its own devices. In one far corner, arum lilies grew against a low stone wall, spearing the sky with their green hearts and yellow tongues. They were her mother's favorite flower, and something about their creamy simplicity made Sarah feel a little better. As if by sitting near them, she was sharing something with her mother.

They made the corners of her eyes prick, it was true, but after a while she stopped feeling so sad, and instead she talked to the flowers in the same way she had spoken to her mother when she'd come home from school. She shared her thoughts and her worries, until her tongue fell as silent as the lilies'. After that she felt a little better.

A few bees swirled dazedly around the tall lilies, pausing every so often to crawl along the cool marble throats of the flowers. Her mother had always loved bees, Sarah remembered. She would tell Sarah that bees were good at keeping secrets, that they carried the dead across from this world to the next. All kinds of nonsense Sarah had hardly believed back then. She wondered now if any of it was true. After all, the world was more magical than she'd ever realized.

One bee landed near her. Sarah paused in her work and stared at it. "And if I told you my secrets," she whispered, "what would you do with them?"

The bee neatened its antennae, then flew off toward the forest.

Sarah turned back to her work. She dug away with her trowel, tidying rows and filling a rusted, decrepit wheelbarrow with weeds. Despite the cold, she was sweating. It was harder work than she was used to, but at least the rain had stopped, and the clouds were thinning and giving way to a faint, watery sunshine.

"I think I'd rather be back at school," she said to the flowers as she slammed her trowel into the earth and a clump of cold, wet soil rocketed into her eye. "Ugh." Sarah leaned back and shook the dirt out of her face. And what was going to happen with school? Her father couldn't have planned on leaving her here for good, cut off from the world, to grow old and mad like Nanna.

She hoped.

Thinking about her father made Sarah's chest go tight and hot. *I miss you*, she thought, *but I don't even know if you miss me.* She had no idea where he was—anything could have happened to him. She remembered the way he'd been before they left to come here. How he'd been all wild about the edges, like a dog who'd missed too many dinners.

Who was making him food now? He never remembered to eat—it was always Sarah who had to remind him. The thought made Sarah's heart feel small and scared. And maybe he'd lied to her about how things were going to get better. He'd said everything was going to go back to normal, but instead he'd left her here, with this broken magic.

He had to come back for her. If he was gone—gone the way her mother was—there might be no escaping, ever. He might have left her here for good. That thought was so enormous, so terrible, that Sarah had been skirting it for days, pretending it wasn't really sitting in the middle of her mind like a sharp rock. There was no running away from it now. It was too late;

she'd looked at that rock and she couldn't unsee it now, or pretend that it didn't exist.

She had no idea where her father was, or what had happened to her mother.

Without them, she was truly alone. Nanna hardly counted, since there was not the slightest hint of grandmotherliness about her at all, and Sarah didn't know if her other grandparents were even alive.

A hot prickle filled Sarah's eyes, and her lip began to tremble. She missed her parents. She missed them so much that it made her throat tight and her whole chest feel like someone had wrapped rubber bands around it until she could hardly breathe.

A sound of feathers brushing together made her turn quickly, wiping her face as she did. She didn't need anyone feeling sorry for her—or worse, feeling nothing at all.

"Oh, it's just you." Sarah scowled at the raven and tried to keep the quiver out of her voice. "You're sneaking up on me now."

"So I am. How did you hear me?"

"I don't know. I just did." She shook her head. "Raven, I need to know . . . is my mother dead?"

The raven didn't answer her directly. Instead it pecked at the ground, as if it had been distracted by plump, wriggling worms. But the earth in this patch was empty. Sarah knew, because she'd just been digging it over earlier. The raven was trying to ignore her. Perhaps the question made it uncomfortable.

"Do you know?" Sarah prodded at it with a wisp of old

grass, and the raven hopped back, feathers ruffled. "You don't, do you?"

The raven clacked its beak. "Of course I do. I certainly know more than a little monster of a girl like you."

"So tell me."

The raven puffed up its breast, and gave a sigh that sounded far too human. "She's not dead yet. But like all creatures, she will have her allotted span."

Sarah frowned. *Whatever that means.* The curse, of course—but what about it? It was all too complicated and messy. It made her think of the time when her mother had tried to take up knitting and how that sad little ball of wool (which was supposed to have become a scarf) had become a tangle of knots and bits of dirt, oddly intertwined with a small key that didn't fit any of the locks in the house. The curse was like that—it had turned something soft and jewel-bright into a snarled mess of filth. The thing was to find the loose ends and slowly unpick it. To try to find a truth in the lies, and smooth it out and follow where it led her. "And . . . my dad?"

It occurred to Sarah that the truth might not be something she wanted to hear, and she swallowed, waiting for the answer.

The raven calmly straightened its feathers with its sharp beak.

Impossible thing! Sarah tried for a different thread. "What happened to my grandfather—now that my mother is gone, is it happening to my dad?"

"Undoubtedly," said the raven. "He will begin to change, faster and faster, until there is nothing human left in him at all, except for the memories of the man he was."

"Can—if he falls in love with someone else? Someone who loves him back? Could that save him?"

"By the terms of the curse, only the first love counts." The raven looked down its thick beak and prodded at the ground, as if it couldn't face Sarah. "I'm sorry."

Sarah's trowel fell from her numb fingers to land on the soil with a soft *thunk*. "But why did he bring me here, then—why leave me and run away?"

"Perhaps he did not want you to see the change," said the raven. "Humans are such prideful things."

"We have to stop it," Sarah said. "We have to find my mother and make her go back to him and—"

"And what?" cawed the raven. "Keep him in an iron cage and feed him scraps? Your mother did right, leaving him. It's better than what Inga did, too scared to run, too scared to change."

"What do you mean, change? You said the curse would kill her. Now you say it won't—or is it all lies?" A little bit of hope grew in Sarah. Perhaps her mother was out there still, waiting to come back one day.

"I never lie," said the raven. "The terms of the curse are . . . complex. Even if your grandmother falls out of love, she has to stay, unless she wants to be turned. If she leaves, she changes too. The witch who decided the terms thought them most amusing and ironic at the time—" The raven suddenly clicked its beak shut, as though it was stopping itself from saying more.

"She turns too? Into a beast?" Was that what had happened to her mother? It was better than death. It had to be.

"No," said the raven. "Not a beast. But death will come to her, sooner than you think."

It was too much. Curses on curses. Sarah stood and slapped the mud off her knees. Enough was enough. Her father hadn't gone to some special hospital to get better; her mother wasn't going to turn up out of the blue and pretend that nothing had happened. The whole mess felt like a nightmare, but Sarah had finally realized that it was real. And no one was coming to save her.

There was no way to find the truth in all these tangles. And what would she get for it if she did? A monster for a father, and a mother who had left her.

"Right," she said. "I'm leaving." The tears had all dried up, and in their place was a hopeless, hard anger. She marched toward the gravel road that her father had driven down. The raven flew after her, wings clapping awkwardly.

Gravel crunched like dry cereal under Sarah's sneakers. No one called out after her, screamed at her to return. The only other sounds were the hushing of the leaves, the slow flap of the raven's wings, and the muted calls of the birds in the forest. Sarah walked for an hour, following the deserted road hemmed in by trees, putting the castle far behind her. The raven followed and said nothing, until Sarah rounded a curve in the road and stopped, her heart plummeting like a rock tossed into a still pond.

The raven cawed once, an apologetic sound, and flew off.

Ahead of Sarah stood the crumbling castle, overgrown with ivy and moss, outlined by the red light of late afternoon.

There was no escaping the forest, it seemed. Not without a guide.

+{ —➤•✦⇦— }+

The rest of the week, Sarah moved in a haze, only half aware of what was going on around her. She ate breakfast, tended the gardens, helped feed her grandfather at night. Her skin was numb, her brain bundled up in fog.

She didn't speak to Nanna or to the raven, just nodded dully and did what she was told. At night she sat on her bed, Steg and Hedge on her lap, a book balanced open. The words would swim in front of her eyes. No matter how hard she tried, it seemed not a single line would stay still, would make its way into her brain. When she felt like crying, she would cup her hand over the little hard nugget of the silver bear on its chain, and push until it felt like the tiny animal was clawing into her chest.

It was on the seventh day that she finally spoke again.

Sarah rammed her trowel into the ground—she'd cleared most of the castle vegetable gardens by then, and had been in-structed that her next task was to try to bring order to the black-berry canes on the far side of the clearing. When she spoke, the words felt thick and dusty, all crammed up in her throat like balls of old newspaper. "What about me?" she croaked.

The raven, which had been pecking delightedly at a stringy earthworm that Sarah had turned up while digging, paused and looked at her. It ruffled its feathers once, gave the earthworm a last jab, then hopped up onto the nearest handle of the wheelbarrow. "What *about* you?"

"When do I turn into a beast?" she asked softly. "When I fall in love?"

The raven was silent.

"Well," said Sarah, looking around at the new-turned earth, the bundles of dying weeds, "I won't let it happen. I'll never let it happen. And I won't let Dad stay a beast. And I *won't* be lied to."

"If you say so," the raven cawed sadly, and flapped off over the trees until it disappeared like a melting snowflake.

Sarah stood up and shivered. Her jacket lay folded on the low, tumbled remains of a wall, and after a brief hesitation, she grabbed it and pulled it on. It left her feeling hot, but Sarah knew that where she was going, she'd need it. She'd stuffed woolen gloves into the pockets, and a narrow scarf. Perhaps, underneath the stumbling zombie she'd been for the last few days, the real Sarah had been planning this all along.

Sarah grinned to herself, even though a ripple of shivers spread in circles down her shoulders and back. *I'll find them. I'll fix it.*

The raven had told her not to go to the Within, that the witches were all gone and no one could help her family now, but Sarah no longer believed this. She'd noticed that the raven told her only what it wanted her to know. It was Nanna's creature, but it also wasn't. Captive and spy, it played its own games, Sarah thought as she set off into the forest.

The trail was easy enough to spot, and she followed it, avoiding the garlands of webs and the spikes of the low branches, always listening for the faint trickle-rush of water that would tell her she'd reached the river she wasn't to cross.

She followed the cold, the puff of her breath, and the wet-black trunks of the pines. Animal tracks zigzagged through the undergrowth, confusing her steps, but she carried on, teeth clenched with determination.

✦⟶ ━━➤⋯⟨━━ ⟵✦

Sarah was lost. She turned around, shoving branches out of her way and panting. "Stupid." She ducked to avoid a particularly low-hanging tangle of twigs. "Tree." A bundle of pine needles scratched against her cheek. "Thing." She wasn't upset yet—at least, not upset enough to start crying—but she could feel herself getting more and more nervous, her heart going faster. What if she stayed lost forever—starved to death in the forest?

Or got eaten by something?

Were there wolves in the forest—or just beasts?

"Raven!" she yelled.

The forest muffled her call, and all she heard back was the faintest hush of the last withered leaves rubbing softly together, like a witch's hands. *At least I'm close to the center, I think.* The forest borders were home to a variety of trees, but when the raven had led her to the river's edge, the forest had been given over completely to the pines and their jagged needles and cones, their sharp resinous smell. The dark heart of the forest.

She backed out of the tangle she was in and glared at the branches. "Fine," she said. "Have it your way." There had to be other routes in.

Silence fell around her with the light, swirling snow. Sarah looked up, her breath misting out from her mouth like dragon smoke. Tiny flakes were dancing their way down through the branches. And then, ever so faintly—a thin splashing noise, like a running tap in someone else's house.

Gotcha.

She took another path between the trees, following the sound as it grew. Every now and again small flurries of snow twisted down through the branches like frozen dandelion seeds and covered her faint footprints.

Finally the trees parted, and the forest opened out to a small bank leading to a black, icy river. It wasn't the same part she'd been to before—this section was rockier, and green-black water spilled over several little ledges to create a series of riffles and rapids. Icy froth churned and collected in the whorls.

There's no way I'm getting across this. There were some slippery-looking rocks that spiked up through the tumult, but they were like rotted black teeth, and far apart. The river was wider than she'd remembered. *Admit it, Sarah, it was a stupid idea anyway.*

Instead of admitting anything to herself, Sarah shuffled closer to the bank and peered down. The drop was steep, and here and there the river had eaten away at the sides to form a precarious overhang. She edged back. "Blast." There was no way to cross the churning river.

A long, low growl sounded behind her, and Sarah froze. Her breath steamed, her whole body shook, but she couldn't move.

Silence.

Just when she was ready to relax and turn around, the growl came again. Closer. Sarah squeezed her eyes shut. *Oh please, please don't be real.* Very, very slowly, she began to turn around. Her heart was knocking out a beat so loud and fast she half expected the forest to be shaking along with her. She stared at the forest edge, at the flickering blackness, saw nothing, and let go of the breath she'd been holding.

It lunged out of the shadows, bursting from between the trunks, high-backed and shaggy as a wolf, but with round golden eyes in a squat bearlike face. Its ears were sharp and pricked, and behind them curled iron-gray horns.

"Oh," squeaked Sarah. There was nowhere for her to go—the river was at her back, and the beast before her. It was drown in freezing water or have her throat torn out. She'd read somewhere once that if a wild animal charged, you should stay perfectly still, but she wasn't exactly sure if this really worked, and more importantly, if it worked for beasts of the magical persuasion. She shut her eyes and tried not to scream.

The beast galloped toward her, paws slamming against the ground, shaking the snow down from the nearby pines. It plunged closer and closer.

And stopped.

It sniffed loudly. A stinking blast of its breath burned against Sarah's face, strong enough to ruffle her hair back. The beast panted and sniffed. The thick, meaty reek enveloped Sarah, almost making her gag. It reminded her of that smell in the shed, of Grandfather.

Sarah wanted to whimper, could feel the whimper building up inside her. *Don't let it know you're scared, don't let it know you're scared.* She kept taking shaky little breaths and hoped that the beast would get bored and go.

"Away with you," called a slow, drawling voice. A familiar voice.

Alan?

Sarah's eyes flew open. She was face-to-face with the beast, its golden eyes as big as apples staring into hers.

The beast grunted, sending another fiery blast of its breath over Sarah's face, then drew away, as if uncertain.

"I said away," Alan continued, patient and amused. "Come now, there's a good boy. She's no good for eating. A stringy thing. You go catch this instead." There was a whistling noise, followed by a thump; the beast turned its head and, after a second's thought, raced away.

"There goes my supper, then," said Alan, standing barefoot in the snow, still wearing a sweater with no shirt underneath and dirty trousers. He'd added a long green-and-blue scarf to the mix, and it trailed behind him, the ends soggy and dark. With a sweeping movement, he held out one hand. "Seems our forests have met," he said. "Or you took a wrong turning."

Sarah's shoulders loosened. She took another deep breath just to reassure herself that she could still, in fact, breathe, and turned her head slightly.

The beast was growling and hunched over, worrying at something on the ground.

"How—"

"Rabbit," said Alan.

She kept looking, unable to drag her gaze away. This creature was smaller than the beast below the castle walls, she was sure of it, and its fur was thicker. On its legs were no marks, no broken chains. *Not Grandfather, not him at all.*

Another thought was worming into her head, and she pushed it down and away.

"Come along." Alan's voice was soft, but not whispery or scared, just the sort of firm voice that some people have, people who work with frightened things—animals or people. "Best move on before your friend there is done with his meal."

Sarah nodded. Her feet wouldn't move. She was half certain that if she took a step, the spell the rabbit held on the beast would break, and it would come charging for her again. *The longer you stand here, the more likely that is. So move.* With another quick huff of breath, Sarah slid her toes through the snow. After the first few shuffles, the rope of fear hobbling her snapped, and she was able to move again. She walked toward where Alan stood, watching the beast feed.

Alan glanced at her once and nodded sharply. "Well done," he said as he took a step back. "Keep your eyes on it always, until it's gone from sight. Don't turn your back on it."

Together they went into the forest, into the protection of its trunks and deep, still places. They didn't say anything. The seconds tapped out in heartbeats, until finally there was no sign of the river clearing between the trees, or any faint rushing call of the water. The beast was out of sight.

Sarah wasn't sure if she should speak or if the sound of her voice would bring the beast after them again, so she kept close to Alan, following the small commands he gave with his fingers—a flick to turn here, a palm held up to stop—until finally he brought them out to a pathway between the trees. It wasn't the road that led to her grandmother's castle, but it was wider than the deer tracks that the raven had led her down.

"We should be safe here," said Alan. "The beasts don't like the old roads, so they tend to stay clear of them. Too open. And besides, you could meet anything on an old road."

"Thanks," Sarah said. "For saving me back there. And I'm really sorry you lost your supper."

Alan blinked. "Maybe I didn't save you at all," he said. "You never know what beasts want."

"Okay, well, thanks anyway, you know."

"Now," said Alan, as they stepped into the clear space. The trees were changing again; white-limbed birches appeared, and small sharp-leaved bushes, and spindly alders, last season's catkins crumbling on the ground. "Why would you be so far from your home, and so close to the Within?"

Sarah tripped over a hidden root and stumbled against him. "I—how do you know about the Within?"

Alan frowned. "How do you?" He helped her upright, and dusted her hair. "Twigs," he said.

"I hate it when people do this," Sarah said. Now that her heartbeat had gone back to normal, the meeting with the beast was beginning to feel like a nightmare, something unreal.

It didn't help much that Alan was patting at her head. It made her feel like someone's grubby cousin. It was humiliating.

"Do what?" he said.

"Answer all my questions with questions."

"Do I?"

"Argh." Sarah loosened her scarf a little; it was beginning to feel like it was strangling her. Her skin was prickly and sweaty with heat, even though her feet were frozen lumps. *Great. Please don't let me be getting sick.* "You're"—she huffed—"improbable. And I'm far from home because my father brought me here to this *place*."

"And why would any father do that to a daughter?" Alan said. He was walking alongside her now, no need for him to lead the way.

"Exactly. Why?" Sarah sniffed. "It's going to sound like I'm making this up, but the truth is—well, I don't know." *And just how much would Alan believe?* If she told him what she really thought, he'd probably think she'd gone mad. Or that she was just a little kid, playing at make-believe. Then again, he was rather odd himself. *And he knew about the Within, so maybe he believes all this stuff about witches.* "I think my father brought me here because he's cursed, and he's scared. I think."

Alan stopped and turned to look at her. He was chewing at one corner of his upper lip, and his brow was furrowed in concentration. "Cursed?"

"I know. It sounds so stupid if I say it out loud." Sarah shoved her hands into her pockets. "But there's nothing else that explains it all. Unless I'm going mad or something."

"If he was cursed, why would you be going to the Within?"

"Oh." She scuffed the loamy earth of the track, shifting the dirt around in an arc. "Well, I had this idea that, if it's all real, if there's really a curse, then maybe I could . . . ask for it to be taken off." She felt the tips of her ears now, they'd gone from freezing-burning to just plain burning. Any minute now he was going to burst out laughing, start mocking her for being a stupid little kid.

"The witches are gone," Alan said after a while. "And no one can get into the Within."

It wasn't exactly the reaction she'd been expecting, and he sounded so serious, like he'd given a lot of thought to this kind of thing before. "If no one can get in, then how can you be so sure they're gone?" Sarah snapped. "Anyway, the raven never said anything about not being able to get into the Within, it just said not to try."

Alan narrowed his eyes. "You've been talking to ravens, have you?"

"Just one. I don't make a habit of it."

"A white one." He sounded angry and amused at the same time, like he couldn't decide exactly how to react. Like he was putting the final pieces in place on a huge, complicated puzzle, only to find the picture was of an unmade puzzle.

"Yes, it's my grandmother's or something. I don't really know."

Alan blinked. "Your grandmother—" He laughed. "Oh. I suppose that makes us mortal enemies."

"What?" Sarah took a step away from him, ducking a little as if he was going to grab her by the scruff of her neck and haul her off to be tortured. He didn't do anything of the sort, of course, which left her feeling more than a little foolish. "What are you talking about—mortal enemies? You mean we're supposed to be facing off against each other with swords or something?"

He laughed again, and shook his head. "We need to talk," he said. "And I need a brandy." Alan walked away, the tails of his scarf flapping against his back, his bare feet as silent as cat paws. "Come along if you're going to come along, or go to your left, and if you strike true you'll find your castle, princess."

There was no denying the feeling that tugged at her. Of course she wanted to know more. And she would far rather follow Alan into the forest just to get a glimpse of the truth than set off back to the castle and all its complicated lies.

"I'm not a princess," Sarah said. And she set off after him.

IN WHICH MOST OF THE TRUTH IS TOLD

THE DIRT ROAD led them to a cottage set in a small open clearing. The aspens fell away to reveal a simple A-frame house with a wide front porch shadowed by a drooping shingle roof. The wood planks were black, streaked with the violent green of moss. Even the roof was covered with its own miniature forest of bracken and red ferns.

Stumps spattered the clearing, and a covered lean-to against one side of the cottage was stacked with amber rounds of new-cut wood. Dead grouse hung from one stunted tree, their feathers fluttering stiffly in the wind.

To one side of the cottage, a small vegetable garden was kept tended. The white ribs of winter kale were bright against the dark, dark green of their leaves.

A streamer of smoke trailed from a thin, crooked chimney into the crisp air.

"Is this yours?" Sarah asked.

"It is and it isn't." Alan opened the door and mock-bowed, ushering her in. "Beauty before age."

"It's the other way around, you ninny," Sarah said as she stepped into the cottage. It was warm. The air smelled of sage and woodsmoke and cat fur. She peeled off her gloves and shoved them into her pocket.

Behind her, Alan closed the door. "Apologies for the lack of light," he said. "You get used to it soon enough."

"It's not that dark." Sarah took in the kitchen table, cluttered with bowls and bundles of herbs; the collection of glass carboys in a corner, filled with pale gold liquid; and a ratty couch that looked like it had been dragged straight out of the occasional dumping ground of the Not-a-Forest. Alan had covered it up with a crocheted blanket in rainbow zigzags, like something someone's granny had made. The colors glowed. Berry reds and deep sea blues and pine greens and daisy yellows. "It's not dark at all."

Alan frowned. "Suit yourself." He pointed at the couch. "Sit. Tea, and then we talk."

Sarah didn't mind the idea of sitting, especially as it was toasty and comfortable in the little cottage. It shouldn't have been—after all, it was little more than a run-down hut in the woods—but it *felt* comfortable. It felt safe. She toed off her sneakers and curled up on the couch.

Alan hummed as he set out cups and gave the saucers a

final quick wipe with a dishcloth. He was frowning in concentration again.

Watching someone make tea shouldn't be this interesting. Sarah leaned an arm on the back of the couch and kept studying him anyway. She felt she almost understood the breathless glee of her classmates as they passed around pictures of their idols and whispered stuff about *amazing arms* and *cutest smile.* Not that Alan was like those cheesy-grinned mannequins. He was different.

"How do you like your tea?" Alan asked without looking up.

"Um, milk, please, and two sugars."

He paused. "I've no milk and no sugar."

Sarah grinned. "You don't often have guests, I suppose."

"I once did." Alan switched the cups around. "And now I don't." He ducked down and rattled about in the cupboard. "Ah." He came back up with a dusty bottle of honey-amber liquid.

Sarah supposed that was the brandy. "None for me."

"I wasn't offering, you daft child." He slugged a generous helping into one cup, just as the kettle on the hob began to scream a fine jet of steam from its spout. "I've some condensed milk," he said. "How about that?"

It sounded reasonable enough, Sarah thought, like premixed milk and sugar. "Why not?"

"Yes. One would think it would be more popular, really." Alan poured the tea, then poked holes in his tin of condensed milk and poured a fine trickle into Sarah's cup.

A moment later, Sarah was holding her condensed-milk

tea in her hands. He had served it in a very fine china set, of the type that elderly aunts used when important visitors sat in the front room and talked about weather.

"So." Alan took a seat in the rocking chair, and perched there like an angular pelican. "You're Inga's grandchild." He put one foot to the floor and gently set the chair rocking. "Inga's grandchild, of all people."

"Yes. How is that important? I mean, you said we're mortal enemies." Sarah took a hesitant sip of her tea. It tasted like a toothache. "Are you trying to poison me with the condensed milk?"

"No," said Alan absently. He took a gulp of his brandy-laced concoction and shuddered. "With the tea, actually."

Sarah looked down in horror. The tea in question *was* unbearably sweet, but that was about it. She wasn't really sure what poison was supposed to taste like, though. *Maybe he put the condensed milk in to hide the taste of arsenic. Or something.*

"I'm kidding," Alan said. "Drink the tea."

"Er," said Sarah. "Maybe later. First, tell me why we're mortal enemies."

"Because." Alan hurriedly took another swallow. This time the shudder seemed to travel right down his legs. "The witch who cursed your grandparents—I'm her boy."

Sarah set her cup down on the low table in front of her. *Of course.* He hadn't seemed the least surprised by her mention of the Within. He knew how to calm the beasts of the forest, and he could walk between all the different broken-apart woods as if they were all one vast green world. "You're her son."

"I didn't say that. You need to listen to what people say. I'm her boy. I worked for her. I'm her beastkeeper."

"Oh," said Sarah after a while, because she couldn't think of anything else. "Did she keep a lot of beasts?"

Alan snorted. "Cats, mostly. But they saw to themselves. I took care of the hens and the geese. Geese are worse than goats, I'll have you know. And I'm good with herb lore, so if she found any broken animals in the woods, it was up to me to fix them."

"I don't mean hens," Sarah said. Cold pooled in her stomach, like her insides were melting into ice water. "You know what I mean."

"The cursed ones," he said. "I know." Alan shook his head. "She only cursed the one, and that was thousands of years ago, or maybe a hundred. Or maybe ten. Time moves differently here."

"Does it?"

"Time, and space." Alan finished the last of his brandy tea. His eyelids had half closed, as if he were about to fall asleep at any moment. "But you're a smart girl; you'll have worked that out already."

Sarah raised her chin and said nothing. She'd only worked it out when she tried to leave. "So the whole forest is cursed?"

"The whole forest is *magic*. That's hardly the same thing." Alan got up. "Sit tight, and I'll tell you the story, and then you decide what you want to decide."

"Fine." Sarah pulled the blanket around her, and tucked her feet under her knees. *Stay focused*, she told herself. *Listen to him, but assume nothing is true.* A little flare of excitement shot through her heart. The raven had already told her one story—its version of the truth—and now she was going to hear Alan's. Maybe somewhere in the middle of the two tales, she'd find out what had really happened.

"You know what happened to your grandmother and grandfather?" Alan began.

"Yes." In a way, although it was hard to really believe. She made herself say it out loud, just so she could hear how utterly ridiculous it all was. "They were cursed by a witch because she thought they were vain and silly and cruel and they deserved each other."

"Jealousy," said Alan. "It always comes down to jealousy." He sighed and put the brandy bottle to his mouth, but didn't drink, just stared thoughtfully as though he were waiting for Sarah to sort all the truth out for herself.

"You think—oh." She pursed her lips. It made more sense that way. Here were the bits of the story the raven wasn't telling her. The handsome prince should have loved the witch instead of the empty-headed but beautiful princess, and all would have been well. "He probably never even saw her," she whispered to herself.

For the first time she wondered about how that might feel. She'd never considered it before. It must have hurt, to know that someone ignored you because your hair wasn't the right shade, or your nose was too long or too short, or your eyes were ditch-water brown instead of hydrangea blue or vice versa. That all the clever or funny things you knew meant nothing if the mouth that said them had lips that were too thin or not thin enough. And so the prince had married, the witch had placed the curse, and now look where it had gotten them. No one was happy. Sarah glanced up. "She keeps him in a cage, did you know that?"

"So?" Alan blew a soft note over the bottle neck. "All cages have keys."

"Yeah, and this one's around my grandmother's neck."

"And when have you ever known someone to not keep a spare key to something important?" he countered. "Never, that's when." Alan grinned slyly for a second, then grew serious again. "So, you know one version of the story. I'll tell you another. You think it's as simple as punishing two wicked, vain people with eyes for nobody but each other, and mayhap that much is true, but there are always other parts to a story. And in this one, there are two witches."

Sarah leaned forward, her fingers clinging tighter to the armrests. "What do you mean, two?"

"Don't play the fool, Sarah. Your grandmother is not a powerless old woman."

The truth was there. It wasn't as if she hadn't noticed the small magics her grandmother had performed. "She's a proper witch, same as the witch of the Within?"

"Yes. Freya and Inga both grew like willows at the same stream."

"Whatever that means."

"It means that they were raised the same, that they both had magic and learned it from the same man. Their father."

"The raven said they were sisters, but they turned on each other anyway." Sarah stood, her skin shivery with goose bumps.

"Freya was the birth child, and Inga the foster, but they

grew up together, close as two girls can be." Alan paused to watch her through the murky glass of his bottle, as if deciding what to tell her next. "And Inga was the prettier of the two, that much is also a truth, but it wasn't her beauty that grew that wicked sore spot between them," he said.

"So what was?"

"Inga turned her attentions to the wrong person."

Sarah frowned. "That doesn't make sense." She shook her head. "Okay, fine. But then Inga was still a witch, she knew magic, you said. So why didn't she just break the curse herself?" Sarah sat back down, pressing her spine against the couch until the springs squealed in protest.

"Because you can't go around breaking curses willy-nilly. It doesn't work like that. Curses are strict. There are rules to follow and conditions to meet. That's the beauty of them. And why they cannot be broken." Alan set the bottle down next to his empty cup. "Besides, even if it were possible, your grandmother didn't have enough power to do something that big." He steepled his fingers and pressed them against his mouth, watching her. "It's still a love story, you know."

"What is?"

"Your grandfather would never have turned into a beast if he hadn't truly loved Inga." He shrugged one shoulder. "And your father wouldn't have fallen in love with your mother if he had known the truth. Or mayhap he would have. Love is a strange master."

The brandy had loosened all his words.

"When I came to work for Freya, it was all long over, of course. I didn't even know about it. This was when she still lived in the Within, and we hardly stepped into the rest of the forest." He stopped the gentle rocking of his chair and leaned forward across the table, his owl eyes blinking in the murk.

"This doesn't tell me anything new," Sarah said mournfully. "I was hoping you'd explain a way for me to break the curse, and instead you tell me it's impossible."

"Nothing's ever impossible," Alan said. "Just—"

"Improbable, I know." Sarah flapped one hand like she was shooing away a bug. "But that doesn't help me. If I can't break it, I need to make sure it never happens to me." She frowned. "And you're sure my dad didn't understand how the curse worked? I mean, if he did, he was an idiot to go and fall in love."

Or he thought that it wouldn't run to him, that the power of the magic had ended with his mother and father. It hadn't, as it turned out.

Alan laughed. "Let me tell you a story of love," he said. "And maybe you'll understand."

"Go on, then."

"There was once a witch's daughter who hated magic. She hated being alone in the middle of a forest, with no friends for company, with only a measly servant to talk to besides her mother. The witch's daughter grew up and slipped away from witchery as soon as she was an adult. She told the servant to teach her how to walk out of the forest, and because he didn't know any better, he did as she asked.

"She escaped magic and lived in a normal apartment, and went to a normal college. She didn't come back to her mother. The servant, seeing how the mother grieved and grew old and small, went to speak to the daughter, begging her to return. He asked her why she wouldn't come back.

"She told him she didn't like the smell of the forest. The cold and the pines reminded her of her life with her mother in the Within. She was scared that if she went back, she'd never again be free.

"Her mother grew older and meaner and colder inside. Love died, in the slow way that it can. The servant still tried to convince the daughter to return, and to be fair to her, she still loved her mother, but only when she remembered to. Her mind was made up, and she never came back to the forest."

The silence filled up again, not with words but with the squeak of the rocking chair.

"That's pretty sad." Sarah's tea had cooled, and an oily smear swam on the dark caramel surface. Even if it wasn't poisoned, Sarah decided that she really didn't want it now. "But what's it got to do with my grandparents?"

"Well, that's just the thing. You see, curses are wicked. And curses always go in circles. Think of your own story—once Freya had her revenge, she withdrew to the cold and the dark, and paid no more attention to your grandmother Inga and her vain prince than they did to her. And so she'd no idea that they'd had a son and that he'd grown up spoiled and happy, until the day his father turned to a beast and the terms of the curse called Freya back to Inga's side.

"They'd sent their precious son far from magic. From forests and castles and stones as old as the bones of the earth. They sent him past the borderlands, to where magic is kitten-weak.

"The spoiled prince learned a trade and went to classes at

night in a cold brick building, instead of sleeping on rich beds. He left his history behind him and built a life under the smoke and stink of human cities. And there he met a girl who reminded him of the forest, and though it seemed like something out of the fancies of children, they looked at each other and fell in love."

"Oh no," said Sarah. "The girl—she was Freya's daughter." She closed her hands and studied the hills of her knuckles. "They didn't—?" she asked, even though she knew they did. Of course she knew they did. She'd always loved the story of how her parents had met—how they had seen each other across a crowded quad, their eyes had met, and *something* had exploded between them, like an invisible firework. Before, Sarah had thought it was love, but now she was beginning to wonder if curses felt like that when they struck. Maybe it was impossible to tell the difference.

Alan nodded. "They knew nothing of each other's cursed pasts, or how it might trap them in the same circle. It's hardly the sort of thing people think to ask about, though perhaps they should."

She marveled sadly. Her mother, running from witchcraft, and her father, running from curses, and somehow they'd crashed into each other, they'd fallen in love. And eventually, she supposed, they'd found out the truth about each other. "But they seemed so *normal.*"

"It was what they wanted. They kept moving, running. When Freya heard what had happened, she wanted to bring your mother back to the Within, to keep her daughter from the curse that snapped at its own tail. She combed the human cities for her daughter, bringing the cold of the Within right out into the world in her hunts."

"The cold . . ." Sarah ached. Her mother had always run from winter, a fawn racing away from a pack of snowy wolves.

"But Inga was also a witch, and though she couldn't break the curse she was caught in, she had enough power to set her own curse on Freya. Freya was doomed, just as Inga's marriage was doomed."

"Doomed? She killed her?"

Alan shook his head. "She might as well have, I suppose. She bound Freya into the form of a raven until the day she lost what she loved most." He sighed softly, and it took a while for this to sink in.

"That's cruel."

"Each as cruel as the other, curses like circles, each begetting another."

Sarah didn't exactly know what begetting meant, but the concept of it, that the curses all led to more curses, like a spiral of madness, was clear enough.

"And then Inga finally got the truth out of her son, that he'd married none other than Freya's daughter, and the curse closed like a trap."

Sarah kept quiet, frowning. "A raven," she repeated softly. "A white raven." She looked at her knees. "Oh. Oh, how awful." Her hands curled into fists. "That's—then she's also my grandmother. How could they do that to each other?" She raised her head.

Alan shrugged and rocked back in the chair. "The terms were set before you were born. And there was only one thing that Freya still loved, in all the worlds. Your mother's death was the only thing that would make Freya human again." He frowned slightly, and the shadows seemed to dance across his skin, making him look suddenly impossibly unreal and beautiful. "It was an ugly thing, ill-done, but it *was* done."

Sarah shifted. She was emptied out inside, and all the hope she'd had of begging the witches to lift the curse from her family had been replaced instead with a thick, dead nothing. Her family's curses were all twisted up in each other, like strangling vines.

"The raven. F-Freya—" Sarah stumbled over the name. *My grandmother. My* other *grandmother.* "She said that the price of leaving their beasts was that the wives would turn into something, but she wouldn't say what." Sarah pulled her knees up against her face and tried to make the words come out right. "My mother—what has she become?"

The chair's slow creak faded as Alan stopped rocking. He watched her, still frowning. The afternoon had passed almost to twilight, and whatever warmth had filtered in though the two small windows at the front of the house was fast fading.

Sarah found herself shivering again, although this time it was not from the near-constant chill of the forest, but from a nameless fear deep inside her.

"Do you remember when we met?" Alan's voice floated through the spreading grayness.

Sarah nodded. "You said you were hunting. A bird—"

"About so big, yes." Alan spread his thumb and forefinger apart. "A little wren."

There was a thick, salty lump in Sarah's throat, and she had to swallow again and again before she could get her next words past it. "A wren. The ones who leave the beasts become birds?"

"Yes."

Sarah pressed her palm over her mouth and breathed in sharply. It felt like she was storing up air so that she'd be able to dive into a deep lake, so that she'd have time to kick her way down to the mysteries that lay on the lake bed. The birds and the beasts—wild and free, and never able to be together. The beasts would hunt in the woods, and the wrens would sing their hearts out, and the two would never understand each other.

And the louder the wrens sang, the more chance there was that the hunting beasts would find them.

She pictured again the beast in the forest, worrying at the rabbit corpse like a terrier with a rat.

A wren would stand no chance. The beast had been huge— one snap of its jaws, and it would crush the tiny bird, piercing heart and lungs and liver with needles made from its own thin bones.

Just.

Like.

That.

"Oh," Sarah said, and the sound puffed into her palm, was trapped there. That was what would happen if her father and mother ever found each other again. She would die, killed by the one who loved her, by the one she once loved. *And dead beasts stay dead.* It was unbearable. "So cruel."

Alan leaned forward and stretched out one hand to tug at her wrist, to pull her fingers away from her face. His skin was warm and dry, and he touched her arm with a gentle patience, like he was petting a kitten. "Yes," he said, his forest voice filled with the welcoming rustle of leaves.

Sarah stared into his eyes—all she could see now in the deep gloom of the cabin—and they were small amber flames, golden pools deep enough to drown in, the glass-yellow of topaz.

They reminded her a little of her grandfather's beast-eyes. She had to go back to see him, to tell him that she understood everything now and that she was going to find a way to stop it all. To set everything right again.

There had to be a way, no matter what Alan or the raven said.

"I have to go," Sarah said, and pulled her wrist from Alan's fingers and ran out the door.

THE KEY OF HORN

SARAH CREPT BACK into the castle, but it seemed that no one had even missed her. She helped her grandmother feed the beast, all the while staring from one to the other and trying to imagine the young girl Nanna used to be. The handsome boy that the chained and stinking beast must have been, to drive a wedge between the sisters so easily.

I haven't got the whole story, Sarah reminded herself as she slopped the bucket of bones and stewed meat over to her grandmother so she could put it in the cage. There had to be more to it. More to Inga and Freya's tale. She didn't even know her grandfather's *name.*

"What was he called?" she said after her grandmother had

locked the cage again and closed the door on the sorry beast. "When he was still human."

"What does it matter?" Nanna snapped. "He's not now."

"But . . ." Sarah paused, the empty bucket swinging against her knees as they walked, the rust from the handle biting into her palms. "He can still talk and—"

"How do you know that?" Nanna whirled on Sarah, her hard, sharp face like an ax in the moonlight. "Been poking your nose where you shouldn't?"

"No." Which wasn't strictly true, of course, but Sarah thought that since Nanna was one big ball of lies, it really didn't matter. "I thought I heard him say something last time."

Her grandmother sniffed and stood up straight, still keeping one eye on Sarah like a hawk watching a little grass mouse. "Talking doesn't make things human."

Sarah pulled up her courage inside her and managed to say, very quickly, "Well, I think it goes at least some of the way."

"Parrots talk," her grandmother said, after a moment. She looked as surprised as Sarah felt about Sarah standing up to her.

"Nope. Parrots repeat, that's different. You don't have a conversation with a parrot." Sarah looked around, though of course it was night, and the raven was nowhere to be seen. "If someone was once a human and magic turned him into a beast, but he can still feel and think and talk like a person, then what is he?"

Her grandmother's eyes went waxy and cold, as if they'd filmed over with ice, and Sarah took a small halting step backward. "He. Is. A beast," her grandmother hissed. "And nothing else."

Sarah knew better than to carry on arguing, but a flame lit up inside her. Her grandmother was wrong—and she knew it. Sarah knew it too. The man in the cage might be beast-shaped, but he was still a man, like her father was still her father, and the little wren that Alan was hunting was still her mother. Like the raven was her other grandmother.

There had to be a way to set it all right again.

Her grandmother turned around on the path ahead, and gave Sarah a hooded stare. Then, rather unexpectedly, she said, "It's better this way, Sarah." She didn't sound like the crotchety, malicious woman who made her go dig out flowerbeds all day. She sounded like a woman who was tired of carrying bags of groceries down a long road all by herself. Or who was sick of one more load of dirty laundry—as if she was about to cry but knew that if she started, she would never stop. "It's easier if he is a beast, and that's the truth of it."

That night Sarah dreamed of claws and horns and wings, and woke, shivering, to a still, dark castle. It took her a long time to fall back to sleep.

She wanted to dream about her family, about walking with her parents through the park to go feed the ducks on a Saturday morning, or riding their bikes all the way to where the town turned to hillsides. Those were good dreams, and she could have stayed in them and pretended they were real. Instead, she had nightmares of hunts, of cold snow that covered all their bodies like a blanket, until at last all she dreamed of was white silence.

❖ ❖

The following day, after lunch and a few halfhearted attempts at the vegetable patch, Sarah jabbed her trowel into the earth and left it there, like a tiny headstone. She was done with gardening. The raven had been avoiding her all day, as if it knew that Sarah had been told the truth.

The raven might be avoiding her, Sarah thought, but just because her grandmothers were cowards didn't mean she had to be like them. She got to her feet and strode purposefully past the rusting hulks of the cars. This time the scraggly hut behind the castle didn't seem half as threatening. Water still plopped off the ragged bristles of the roof, but the drops made a sad, lonely sound as they dripped into the muddy pools. The door was just a rotten tooth in an old man's mouth, and when Sarah pushed it open, the squeal of the unoiled hinges sounded more like a scared animal than an eerie horror-movie sound track.

"Hello?" she said into the dark. Her voice was a little rough since she'd run most of the way there. She had already faced another, younger beast in the woods, and it *had* scared her. But Grandfather was another story altogether.

He was old, and weak, and his paws were crumpled under his body from lack of use, and all he ever ate were kitchen scraps and bones with all the marrow boiled out.

At the sound of her voice, the lurking shape in the cage

moved, and a moment later, his eyes flashed like lamplights in the dark.

"Hello," Sarah said again, feeling a little foolish now. She pressed one hand to her side to ease out the stitch she'd gotten from running. Her face was crackly like old paper from dried tears, and she could feel long itchy scratches where the trees had slapped at her cheeks. "I've come to talk, if that's okay?"

The silence gathered around the two of them, as her grandfather considered. "Talk," he said finally. His animal mouth made his words sound furred and strange, but at least Sarah could understand him.

She picked her way closer to the cage, and stopped only a few inches from the small door. She crouched down on her haunches. "What is your name?"

The beast frowned, his eyes darkening. It took him a very long time to answer, as though he could barely remember. "Eduard," he said, and seemed surprised at the sound of it, at his own name.

Eduard. Grandfather. He was more than just a beast, and Sarah vowed to herself that she would never forget it. She shuffled a little closer. "I spoke with someone yesterday."

Her grandfather blinked and waited.

"He used to work for the witch who cast the curse on you. He told me the story of what happened to our family."

"Ah," breathed her grandfather. "Alan of the Woods."

"You know him?" Sarah couldn't quite keep the surprise out of her voice, though it did make sense that Grandfather would at least have heard of the witch's servant.

"Not half as well as I would like," he said. "He's a tricksy thing."

"Oh," said Sarah, in a small voice. "How do you mean?"

"He belonged to the Within once, and that means he's more powerful than he pretends."

"He's just a boy."

"And you are just a girl," Grandfather retorted, "but you won't stay one forever."

Sarah's heart gave a frightened little skip, and she shivered. "That's kind of what I came to talk to you about," she said. "The curse. I need to know everything you know about it."

"Why?" he asked sullenly. His teeth were very long.

"Because." Sarah straightened and stood up. "Don't you think it's possible that there's a way to break it?"

The beast growled and made a coughing roaring sound, so that Sarah took a few worried steps out of reach before she realized he was probably laughing. "Of course there's a way," he said. "It's in the rules."

"Well, no one's exactly told me the rules, have they?" Sarah said. She crossed her arms. "So what's the trick?"

"No trick." The beast sat carefully upright, and his chains jangled and clanked, and beneath his crippled paws dry old bones snapped with crickle-cracks. "Only a secret. One that Freya won't tell you."

The raven. Sarah had to find a way to get the raven to tell her how to break the curse. Surely she would do it—after all, she couldn't want to see not only her daughter cursed, but her granddaughter too. "Perhaps I can convince her," Sarah said, confidence bounding up. That was, if she could ever track her down.

"Good luck to you," said the beast. He sounded amused and resigned. "You'll need it, I daresay. It's not like we haven't begged and threatened and wept." He cocked his heavy, maned head and considered her. "You have something of her in your face, and it's true she misses your mother more than she'll ever say. Perhaps, if there's any who could sway her, it would be you." He sneezed, then scratched at his mangy fur, leg thumping and chains ringing. "Go on then, girl—Granddaughter— break her heart, and make her see reason."

"I won't need to go that far, I think," Sarah said. She paused, then stretched one hand between the bars to stroke her grandfather's muzzle. "My parents used to call me Sarahbear," she said softly.

"Sarahbear." The beast rolled it around on his tongue.

Sarah withdrew her hand and set off, determined to wrangle the truth from her raven grandmother, one way or the other. She paused at the door and looked back at the beast in his cramped, sad cage. "It's not fair," she whispered. "That Nanna does this to you."

The beast shrugged. "Perhaps it's all I deserve."

"Do you want me to leave the door open, so you can get fresh air and a little light?" As she spoke, she was already making plans, and plans on top of those plans. Having goals was making her feel less sorry for herself. Her determination to not let this curse get the better of her was keeping her spine straight and her heart fierce. "I can come close it again before Nanna feeds you, so she won't notice it's been open."

"And know that the world exists, and moves on without

me?" The beast settled back down, nose to tail, his horns gleaming in the faint light. "Thank you, no."

And Sarah, who almost understood what he meant, closed the door softly. Before she headed for the castle, she went to the half-dug vegetable patch and took one of the small pieces of chalky stone she'd turned up in her gardening. She tucked it into her back jeans pocket, and began to hum.

⋆⊹ ➣••⋘ ⊹⋆

Typically, the raven was still nowhere to be found. *She's always hovering about when I don't need her.* Sarah skittered through the dark passages and climbed the spiraling staircase up to her room. Everything had been neatly swept and put away. Not by her hands, of course. Nanna's magic at work. Sarah looked around the little turret room. Even though she'd spent her whole life living out of boxes and moving every few months, no room of hers had ever looked less like her own. *I don't belong here.* The thought was fierce. *And I won't be forced to stay.* Alan knew how to get in and out of the forest—that much was true. Next time she saw him, she'd ask him to show her how it was done.

Until then . . . *There are a few things that need doing around here.* Sarah picked up the bundle of candles that Nanna had left on her dressing table, and picked the knot apart. There was a dusty box of matches alongside them. She took one candle, and stuffed a spare and the box of matches into her pocket.

The lamps still guttered in the hallways, but it was time she found out all the secrets Nanna and the raven were keeping.

Nanna was currently in the kitchen—it seemed to be the place she spent most of her time, always busy carving up dead animals to feed to the beast. Sarah had seen her when she'd ventured there to grab a quick sandwich, and Nanna had growled some more instructions about having the vegetable gardens ready.

And now Sarah was ready to sneak through the places she wasn't supposed to go.

Nanna never specifically told me not to wander about the castle. Of course, if she'd known what Sarah was going to do, she might have left more explicit instructions. Sarah ran along the passages until finally she came to the last of the glowing lamps. She lit her first candle and, with a deep breath, stepped into the dark and made a mark on the castle wall with the chalky stone she'd taken from the garden. Her small, rough arrow stood out bright against the dull stone.

The cave smell of old stone grew stronger as she walked, the candlelight bouncing and guttering like a will-o'-the-wisp before her. The single candle was just barely enough to light more than her face and a footstep or two of her path. The shadows seemed all the darker for the little bit of buttery light.

Sarah tiptoed faster, the shadows clinging to her shoulders like shed ghost-skins. A breeze riffled through the hallways, carrying with it the faintest scent of pine needles and forest mulch. It moaned sadly about her legs. "Hush, you," Sarah said out loud, to prove to herself that she wasn't the least bit frightened. The wind obediently quieted down, and soon the only sound was of Sarah's footfalls soft in the castle dust. At every turn, she marked the wall, leaving a trail of chalky arrows behind her.

From the outside, the castle appeared to be nothing more than a single ruined turret, but like the forest, it was bound by its own strange rules. As she'd expected, it was bigger on the inside, full of twists and turns that led into deeper and darker places. Sarah smiled grimly. She was finally beginning to understand the rules of this place, and that took her one step closer to finding an answer.

Sarah found her grandmother's room only after the first candle had sputtered out and she'd had to light the spare, fumbling in the dark. She knew as soon as she stepped in front of it that this was the one. It had a Nanna-ish air to it: imposing and regal. She raised the candle to the polished wood, and the door gleamed deep and blood-dark as fallen berries. The handle stung her palm, it was so cold, but it turned easily, and the door swung open with barely a whisper.

She took a moment before crossing the threshold. Wandering around the castle was one thing, but actually invading her grandmother's private room was another. No excuses would work if she was caught. Sarah cupped one hand around the flame to hide her actions and stepped forward.

No bells rang. No magic spells flared into life. No bats or birds or demonic creatures leaped from the shadows to attack her. Sarah let out the breath she'd been holding. *Of course nothing happened. It's just a room.*

A room far bigger and more lavishly furnished than her own. There was a vast four-poster bed in the center of it, covered in layers of thick blankets and stitched silk. The colors bloomed and gleamed in the orange light. One side of the bed was slightly sunken, but the other half was pristine. Sarah edged to the sunken side, and made for the writing desk that was pushed against the wall there. It stood on spindly curving legs and had a great many drawers. Sarah went quickly through each one and found some old yellowed paper, candle stubs, string, a collection of white feathers tied in a bundle, three pencils worn down too small to hold, a handful of coins with holes in them, and a monogrammed handkerchief with lace edges.

Sarah finally found what she'd been searching for when she pulled a small carved wooden box out from under the bed. It was patterned with blue and green vines, with tiny birds—each no bigger than a baby's pinkie nail—hidden in the twists and coils. The paint was faded and mostly rubbed away to the bare wood, but it must have been beautiful when it was new. It had no lock, but it took Sarah only a few moments before she worked out how to open it. She had to run her fingers along the vines in a certain way, and press two birds at the same time. The box clicked in a most satisfactory way, and the lid sprang open.

Inside was a folded square of silk, water-spotted and crumbling, and on that lay a small key, carved from dark horn and no longer than her finger. It looked too small to open the cage, but it was a match to the ivory one her grandmother wore around her neck.

Sarah grinned and snatched it up.

+⁝——❧··☙——⁝+

Her grandmother caught her just as she was headed to the main castle door. Luckily Sarah had long since looped the key on the little teddy-bear chain, and now it pressed against her breastbone, digging into her skin like a sharpened claw.

She felt her grandmother's fingers catch at the back of her neck seconds before the old woman spoke. "And where do you think you're off to?"

"I—I still haven't finished the vegetable garden," Sarah said. Her heart pounded so fast in her chest she was sure it was about to bounce right through her rib cage and go hopping off into the forest like an India rubber ball. Nanna was sure to know where she'd been, and what she'd taken.

The fingers released their grip, and Sarah risked a backward glance.

Her grandmother was frowning, and wisps of her white and gray hair had come loose to frame her face, echoing the lines that bracketed her pinched mouth. "Hmph," she said. "Well, get going, then. And don't be late for dinner."

"I won't." Relieved to have escaped so lightly, Sarah fled around to the back of the castle. She looked this way and that. No one was watching her. No one had followed.

Cautiously, Sarah approached the hut. Dusk was falling in long silvery tiger stripes, and the first of the forest owls were already swooping over the clearing, their wings like sails. A few night insects were beginning to burr and creak, and the last of the day birds was sleepily calling. Sarah shoved open the door and hurried inside. Quickly as she could, she pulled her silver necklace free and undid the clasp, and slid the horn key off the chain.

"Back again?" growled the beast.

"Shh," Sarah replied. "Quick." She knelt before the cage door. In her hand, the key looked disturbingly small. Too small for the lock it was meant to fit, and for a moment she wondered if she'd wasted her time today, if all this had been for nothing. But the tiny horn key trembled and grew, and before she could think twice, Sarah was unlocking the door.

She hopped back and pulled it open.

The beast stared at Sarah.

Sarah stared back. "Well?" she whispered. "What are you waiting for?"

"Where did you get that key?" he said.

"Does it matter?" Sarah felt herself flush. Even though she was doing it for a good cause, she couldn't help feeling a little bad about stealing. It just wasn't something in her nature. "Bring your paws closer." He did, and Sarah unlocked the first of the manacles. The chains fell dead and heavy into the rotted straw and bone chips. "Come on, and the other. Don't you trust me?"

"Trust *you*?" He laugh-roared. "I could bite your head off if I wanted."

"But you won't." Sarah inserted the key and twisted. The manacle had to be forced open, it was so rusted.

The beast stretched out his paws, shaking off the last of the chains. "How can you be sure?"

"Because." Sarah got up from her knees and waited for the beast to squeeze through the tiny door. "You're still a human," she said, as he wriggled first one shoulder through and then the other. "You talk, you think, you reason. You're just beast-shaped, is all."

"So trusting," said the beast, when he had finally slithered free. Out of the cage, he seemed bigger, fiercer, his mane rippling and lamp-eyes flashing.

Sarah noticed that the tips of his horns were wicked sharp, and his old yellow teeth were even longer than she'd remembered. "Maybe." She turned her back on the beast, and flung open the shack door. "And maybe that's a good thing, you know?"

Her grandfather fell silent as the greeny dusk light flooded in. He paused to nudge Sarah's hand with his wet nose, as if to say thank you, and then, with a giant leap, he bounded out of the confines of his home, and streaked out toward the gloamy forest without a backward glance.

Sarah swallowed. In her hand the key began to shrink, until it was once again just a little twist of blackened horn. She held it tight and walked out, and hurled it far away, to be lost forever in the weeds and rocks.

There. It's done. And now all that's left is to find that stupid raven and get it to talk. A curious thrill spread out all over her body, making her scalp and fingers and toes tingle. "Raven!" she yelled. "Freya! *Grandmother!* Where are you?"

But it was not the white raven grandmother who came at her beckoning. Instead it was Inga, wrapped in her cloak of iron-dark fur, her hair streaming behind in a storm cloud, who thundered out from the castle. "Foolish, stupid, useless child!" Nanna screeched, as she took in the scene. "Incompetent, liar, and thief! What have you done?"

The tingle died, to be replaced by a sinking fear. "I set him free," Sarah said. "I had to, don't you under—"

The slap cut across her words, her grandmother's palm striking her face so hard it sent her sprawling to the ground, her cheek on fire, fierce tears of pain already gathering in her eyes.

WOODS-WALKING

"GET OUT OF MY SIGHT," Nanna hissed. Her voice stung like a winter gale.

Down on the ground, Sarah slowly lowered her hand, and tried to look up at the woman who was all she had left as human family. Her grandmother's face was hard and cold as a knife edge. Her knitting-needle gaze seemed to stab right through Sarah, piercing to her bones. Sarah rose to her knees. "I'm sor—"

"I don't want to hear it." Nanna's voice was dead, utterly emotionless. "Leave." She turned, and the hem of her fur coat swept bare inches from Sarah's nose. Nanna walked away.

For a few heartbeats more, Sarah stayed on her knees in the tanglehead grass, the dirt blackening her jeans. She dug her fingers into the earth, and fought against the harsh sob that lurched up her body. *I won't cry.* A few more beats, a few more breaths, and Sarah raised her dry eyes. There was no sign now of her grandmother. The dusk had given way to the velvet night, and a half-moon grinned low, just peering over the castle walls.

The night held its breath, and then the first few sounds began trickling back in. The high strange calls of the night birds, the rustling branches, the *click-click* of the things that moved in the dark.

A fox screamed like a ghost-woman, and Sarah jerked. Quickly, she got to her feet and ran for the castle doors. They were closed, and as much as she rattled and banged, they would not budge.

Rage swept over Sarah. This wasn't how family were supposed to treat each other. Her mother would never have locked her out in the cold, no matter what she'd done. This wasn't normal. If this was how her dad had grown up, she wasn't surprised that he'd never wanted to come back here. That he'd never talked about this other family full of cruel magic and lies. He must have been beyond desperate when he'd driven her up here.

Sarah missed him. Missed her mother so fiercely that it made her whole body ache. She wanted them both to come and gather her back into their family and wipe away the awfulness of this year. As if it was a bad dream she'd woken from in the middle of the night, and hot chocolate and warm arms would melt the memory of it.

She slammed her fists against the hard black wood until her knuckles were scraped raw and the bones bruised, but no one came. She put her back to the vast door and, shivering, looked out onto the wall of the forest. It flickered green and black and silver, the leaves like dancing glass.

It was that, or perhaps spend the night in the revolting shack where Grandfather had been caged. In the morning, maybe Nanna would see reason. Sarah curled her hands into fists and marched straight to the moonlit forest. Her eyes slowly adjusted. Under the light of the half-moon, she could see fairly well. The shadows were deep blue as spilled ink, the edges of the leaves limned silvery sharp against them, but she could make her way through the undergrowth.

Even the spiderwebs caught the filtered moonlight and shone.

She walked, hoping to find the wide road that she remembered walking with Alan. He'd help her—let her sleep on the rainbow-throw-covered couch, perhaps even talk to Nanna in the morning.

Only, once again, the forest played its twisting tricks on her, leading her this way and that until her head was too muddled to think straight. All around her the wind whistled, seeming to change direction with every gust. From far away came a lonesome yowling and howling. Some beast was singing through the night.

A deeper song joined the first, and the two creatures yipped and ululated. Even the shrieking foxes were drowned out.

Sarah took another turn and pushed her way through a stand of whippy saplings, only to see the low stone wall of the vegetable garden, with the castle hulking overhead. Her heart sank.

Sarah sat down on the garden wall and put her face in her hands. The night had grown chillier, and the traipse through the forest had left her sweaty. Her soaked clothes cooled. She shivered in the dark, her hands pressed hard against her cheeks.

Move, she thought. *You can't sit here feeling all sorry for yourself. What good's that going to do?* She got to her feet and trudged to the back of the castle. It looked like she had no choice but to spend the rest of the night in the filthy, stinking hut.

She stopped when she came to the rusted-out car, with its sleepy hens clucking softly to themselves. The hens would be warm. And while the car might be full of chicken poo and old feathers, it was a more appealing bed than the hut. Carefully, she clambered in and sat down in the midst of the surprised hens. They squawked and shifted in consternation, then seemed to decide that she was no great threat and tucked their heads away.

There's no way I'll get any sleep in here, Sarah thought, just before her chin nodded onto her chest and her eyes closed. A moment later she was softly snoring.

+}— ⟶>··⟨⟶ —}+

The light stung her eyes. Even with her eyelids tight shut, the morning sun seemed to cut right into her head, red and harsh. Sarah curled up smaller, shifting an indignant hen, and covered her face with her arms. Her throat hurt. Her knees ached. Her skin was shivery and damp.

Finally she couldn't ignore the curious pecking of the hens, and Sarah squinted one eye open and groaned. It was the crack of dawn. Not that the resident rooster had noticed. He'd started crowing hours before the sun rose.

"I will eat you," Sarah mumbled. "I swear it." Her voice was little more than a croak, and talking made it feel like someone had forced razor blades down her throat. She rubbed at the sleep in her eyes and sat up slowly. Her head spun.

A strange gurgling noise woke her properly. It had come from the vicinity of her stomach. Sarah hugged her knees and tried to tell herself that it was going to be all right now. Her grandmother wouldn't leave her to starve out here. Slowly, moving like an old person, she uncurled and made her way back to the castle door.

The wood gleamed blackly in the red dawn. With a lump in her throat, Sarah raised her aching fist to knock again.

Again the door stayed immovable, and no one answered. She'd been thrown out for good, and even the raven had abandoned her. "At least give me my stuff!" she yelled, but it came out more like a sad little croak, and she was certain no one heard her.

Sarah went back to the hens and sat there, wondering what to do next. Thanks to the rooster and the cold and her own despair, she hadn't managed to sleep well, and she was understandably tired. So it wasn't long before once again she drifted back into a feverish sleep, her dreams stippled with sunlight.

⁎⟶⟩⟨⟵⁑

In the dream, Alan was leaning on the windowsill of the car, peering in at her. His arms loose, his fingers almost brushing her nearest knee. "Nice bed you have there," said Alan.

"It's not a bed, you idiot. It's a worn-out piece of junk." Even in the dream, her throat felt all scratchy, but at least the words came out clear. Her nose was running too, and she tried to surreptitiously sniff and wipe, without looking like a baby.

"So why are you sleeping in it?"

"Long story," Sarah said. "I may have set my grandfather loose, and that may have upset Nanna."

"May have?" Alan raised one eyebrow, giving his face a delightfully off-center look.

"Probably did."

"And she punished you by locking you out," Alan said. "And you hope that by now she'll have settled down, and she'll let you back in."

"Something like that." She curled up smaller, sweaty-shivering. "And then the raven will come back."

"And? You suppose that then she'll explain to you how to end the curse, and everything will be right as rain." It was amazing how easily the dream version of Alan understood exactly what was going on. Sarah decided that dream people were much more convenient than real-life people, at least when it came to explaining things.

"Mzagly," Sarah mumbled. The light was hurting her eyes, sending throbbing bolts of pain right into her skull. She felt like she was being boiled in the car.

"Up, girl," said Alan. His voice was louder.

Sarah blinked. Alan was leaning on the windowsill of the car, peering in at her. His arms loose, his fingers almost brushing her nearest knee. He was frowning. "Why are you sleeping in the car?"

"Already explained."

"Not to me you didn't." He sighed. "Come on, you're sick as a dog, and the old bat isn't answering when I knock." He jerked the rusted car door open and carefully tugged her out. "Can you walk?"

"Maybe." Sarah swayed on her feet. "I think so."

Alan frowned again. "This way, then."

Sarah followed him away from the castle. She tried to pay attention to all the paths he took, but it all slopped into a soupy mess in her head. "Why were you at the castle, anyway?"

"Might have been worried about you," he said.

"Might have?"

"Probably was." He gave her a concerned look. "Here. It's not far now. Think you'll make it?"

Sarah nodded, too tired to talk any more, and trudged onward, one foot in front of the other. She reached the cottage in the clearing, and the last thing she remembered was Alan pouring her a spoonful of something sour-sweet.

And then sleep.

⁺⁺ ⟶⟶⟵⟵ ⁺⁺

"Feeling better?" Alan asked Sarah over a breakfast of scrambled eggs and another spoonful of the sour medicine. Her throat was ticklish-sore, but nowhere near as bad as it had been the day before. She could swallow without wincing.

"Yes." Sarah set her fork down. Her head was clearer. She still ached a little all under her skin, but it was the kind of ache she could mostly ignore. "I give up."

"Eh?" Alan paused at his dishwashing, and looked back over his shoulder. "What's what?"

"I give up," Sarah said louder. "I refuse. I'm going home."

"Ah." He set the last dish on the rack and went back to the table. He looked at her, arms crossed. "How do you plan on doing that?"

"You're going to show me." It was right. It was time. She'd done her bit by setting her grandfather free. And now she was going to do exactly what her mother and father had done before her. She was going to leave this crazy forest and all its curses behind. Probably there was no curse, not really—it was all lies and misunderstandings. Her father would be back at home. And maybe her mother too; she wasn't a bird. And her father wasn't a beast. Her eyes stung with tears. "You know how to walk into the Not-a-Forest. You know the way from here to there."

"And back again." One corner of Alan's mouth twitched upward, but he didn't smile. Not quite. "Fine. I'll teach you." He picked up her plate and set it in the sink before heading out into the late-morning sunshine. "Remember what I said before—about how all forests were once one?"

"Yes." They were crossing the little clearing. The grass was withering, and a few dandelions still raised puffy seed heads, but most of the stalks were bare now. "You said they remember."

"That they do." Alan stepped into the shade of the forest and held out his hand. "You just need to walk into their memories, and then you can travel between all the woods in the world, with only a few steps."

"That simple, huh?" Sarah smiled. The tears that had

threatened were drying away now, and she felt that perhaps this was what she should be doing. Something about Alan just made everything seem like it wasn't that bad. His hand was warm in hers, and she felt a calm rightness settling over her.

"It's magic."

"Of course it is." She tugged at his hand. "Show me."

Alan moved in silence, pulling her with him a little deeper into the forest.

"Alan?"

"Shhh, I'm remembering."

Sarah fell quiet, and tried to remember too—the way the little eucalyptus trees grew in shaggy bunches from the sandy soil, and the smell of their leaves. The glint of abandoned rubbish, the tracks left by strangers, candy wrappers and birdsong, and prickly shrubs with papery violet flowers.

Around them, the forest shifted and grew familiar.

"Do you want me to stay?" Alan said, when they stood in the Not-a-Forest. The sky above was as blue and bright and fierce as she remembered, the saplings cast no shadows, and distantly she could hear children shouting, cars humming, sparrows chittering.

No foxes, no snow, no scampering unseen things.

No beasts howling into a frozen night.

"No," said Sarah. She shrugged out of her jacket. "I'll be fine." She smiled at him. "Thanks. You've been the best friend I could ever have had."

Alan looked at her with a fierce solemnity. "You can't have

had many, then," he said, but then he grinned. "Away with you."

Sarah didn't need telling twice. She waved and ran off down the little sandy paths that cut through the Not-a-Forest, on her way home at last.

INVISIBLE FIREWORKS

THE UNMAGICAL HOUSE looked exactly the same. It had the same beige walls, square windows, neatly tiled roof. The grass on the front lawn was clipped down to keep the clover from taking over, and the front door was white and shiny as it had ever been.

There was a red tricycle on the lawn, lying on its side.

Sarah stood at the edge of the road, not quite ready to step onto the lawn and make her way up to the front door. She thrust her hands into her pockets and shivered a little, despite the high sun. Maybe the forest had changed her. It smelled wrong here—too smoggy and thick and greasy. If she opened her mouth, she could taste the exhaust fumes from distant traffic, the overflowing neighborhood trash cans, the chemical choke of household detergents.

She swallowed, and looked again at the red tricycle.

Maybe some neighborhood kid had left it there accidentally. A distant shout followed by laughter made her look up, toward the wall that hid the backyard. A head appeared. Disappeared. Another appeared—a girl's head, blond pigtails flying. Up and down, up and down, the faces came and went.

There were people jumping on a trampoline in her back garden.

The white door burst open, and a woman stared out at her, frowning. "Can I help you?" she called. "Are you looking for Megan?"

"I—" Sarah found she had nothing to say. Her mouth stayed open, but the words all gathered up in her throat and wouldn't come out.

The woman trotted across the neat lawn. As she drew nearer, her frown deepened. "Are you lost?"

"I—" Sarah's mouth snapped shut, and she shook her head. All she wanted to do was get away from here. Her father was gone. No matter what she'd wanted the truth to be, this was reality. She had to face it. There was no going back to a happy family where Mom and Dad loved each other and everything was as safe as houses. There was just this: a strange new family had taken over the unmagical house, and her parents were gone. She was alone.

Sarah stumbled back. "I'm looking for the man who used to live here. He's my, um, uncle."

The woman paused and crossed her arms. "The previous tenants? They've gone, and they didn't even bother to leave a forwarding address. I've a whole packet of mail for them—I was going to return it all to the post office—"

"I could take it to—to him for you."

"But you've no idea where he—oh, never mind." The woman turned away. "Just wait there. It'll take me a few seconds to find it."

Sarah stood motionless, going hot and cold, half watching the bouncing heads over the wall. Her mind was elsewhere. *Letters. Maybe there's something there from Mom.* Her heart beat faster and faster when she saw the woman opening the door again and coming toward her with a plastic grocery bag.

"There you go," she said, and handed the bag over. "You will find him?" she asked, perhaps already second-guessing her decision to simply hand over the mail.

"Yes," said Sarah. She swallowed; the plastic handle was sweaty against the palm of her clenched fist. "You can count on it. Thank you."

As soon as the woman had retreated back into her house, Sarah walked to the Not-a-Forest. At first she moved as unhurriedly as possible, swinging the bag against her legs. But as soon as she was out of sight of the unmagical house, she took a deep breath and sprinted. She needed to see what was in the collection of mail. Even though she thought she'd trained herself to stop hoping for anything, she couldn't help the feeling that rose in her now. She almost couldn't breathe.

In the safety of the first clump of scraggly bushes, Sarah

tipped the letters out onto the ground, and knelt to sort through them.

Boring bill after boring bill, business letters with typed names and addresses and company logos. A whole pack of junk, and not a single message from her mother. The last envelope fluttered from her numb fingers. All Sarah wanted to do was curl herself small.

Everyone was gone.

She couldn't go back to Nanna—her grandmother had made sure of that—and now she really was alone in the world. Sarah was shaking so hard it seemed to her that she'd been caught in a terrible fever, and her throat was hurting again. It was a different kind of hurt this time. A choked little sound burst out of her mouth. She was too upset to even cry.

"Sarah?"

She focused through the haze of unshed tears in her eyes.

It was Alan, peering at her, his mouth turned down in worry. He must have just stepped out of the cover of the trees, because she was certain she'd been alone not a second before.

"You didn't leave," she said. One hand flew briefly to the little bear pendant under her T-shirt.

"Of course I didn't. I wanted to make sure you were safe first."

"Oh." Sarah lowered her hand and looked at the discarded letters at her feet. They covered the tips of her shoes like a tiny snowdrift. "It's all true," she said, very softly. "Everyone is gone, and I'm alone. Of course, you knew it was all true."

"I'll take you back home," Alan said. "Your proper home."

With a small sniff, Sarah took his hand and once again let his magic tug her through from one forest to another. The cold slapped at her face as she left the scrubby tangle of the Not-a-Forest behind and stepped into the heart of the castle's woods. "I haven't got a home." Sarah pulled her hand free. "*She* won't have me back."

"I'll talk to her, "Alan said. "You can wait in my cottage, if you'd rather."

Sarah nodded, and a moment later, the magic had pulled them into the clearing.

+{ —➤••◄— }+

It was dusk when Alan came back.

Sarah had made herself some tea and eaten the fruit he'd left her, and then, because she'd been tired of waiting, had helped herself to a can of spaghetti in tomato sauce, which she felt a little bad about, but not too much. They were friends now, and she knew he'd understand.

She'd even started the fire on her own, and it was going pretty well. She was oddly proud of it. But when he walked in the door, her smile faded. She knew from the look on his face what he was going to tell her. "She said no."

Alan sighed and went to the fire to toss in another log, even though it hardly needed it. A wreath of sparks jumped up the chimney, and a curl of new smoke twined into the room. "We'll give her a few days," he said. "She's not made of stone."

A few days. Here in Alan's cottage. Sarah looked around. Where would she sleep? "Thank you, but I—"

"I'll take the couch," he said. "And I'll make up the bed fresh for you." He gave the fire a last furious jab, then dropped the poker back onto its rack. "I'm sorry." He stood and looked at her. "It's not what you wanted to hear."

"I've got most of the truth. I've tried getting to the Within, stolen a key and freed my grandfather, I've learned how to walk the forest, gone back home . . . and after all this, I haven't solved anything," she whispered. "My family's still missing, still cursed." She swallowed. "*I'm* also cursed, aren't I?"

Alan looked uncomfortable, then gave a small nod, just the barest dip of his head. "Probably." He smiled with one half of his mouth. "If you are, we'll find a way of breaking it."

"How?" Sarah shook her head. "I know that you said I shouldn't, but I am going to go to the Within—it's all I can think of to do now."

Alan stared at her, and his brows pinched together as he considered. "You may be right," he said after a few moments. He ran one hand through his brown curls, and a tiny silver leaf spiraled to the ground. "Then again. You may be wrong, and it may be the very worst thing you could do. The Within is where all the magic comes from. Go there, and the curse will wake in you."

"Will it?"

Alan fiddled with the fallen leaf, twisting it about in his fingers. "To tell the truth, I don't know for sure."

Sarah almost smiled. "Then that settles it. I have to take the chance."

"You don't." His eyes burned like amber glass around candles, bright and warm. "You shouldn't. We'll think of something else, you and I, and I promise this much," he said as he stepped forward to catch her hand, "you won't be alone. I'll be with you."

It was a jolt.

A strange moment when the world stayed exactly the same, and changed forever.

It felt like an invisible firework.

And Sarah's bones shifted just the slightest bit under her skin. She pulled back away from Alan's touch, wrenching her hand free. The room smelled suddenly close and stale and smoggy. She coughed, spluttered.

"Are you going to be all right?" Alan didn't seem offended by her reaction, just concerned.

"I'm fine," she choked out between coughs. "Just too much smoke in here. I need to breathe." Sarah leaped from the couch and flung the door open.

Beyond, the trees danced, green and blue against a sky alive with light. She watched the first stars pinwheel in their courses, and around her the forest came to life in a flutter of scents and sounds. The air cut into her lungs, and she could taste where the castle was from here, could feel the tug of its stones beneath the earth. She looked at her feet, half expecting to see the ground moving, showing her the way back home.

Nothing, just her feet in her socks. Light gray socks with their pattern of pink cat paws along the side. Her mother had bought them for her.

Through the toes of the socks, her feet looked wrong. Too flat and human, no good for running or hunting, no good for padding soft as falling feathers through the crackling leaves.

"Oh no," said Sarah. "Oh no. Please, no."

"You're changing," said Alan behind her. "Why are you changing—you're just a little girl—you can't be more than twelve."

"Thirteen," Sarah said, and she wanted to scream. Because when he'd spoken, she'd felt the hunger in her rising. She could smell the grouse hanging limp on the trees, the meat-richness of them, and known. "Stop talking," she said, and ran.

There was no way he'd be able to catch up, Sarah thought as she raced. The trees flickered around her, an impossible blur. She knew instinctively when to duck, to turn, to slip this way instead of that. Beneath her pink and gray socks, the ground was mute.

She'd left her jacket in Alan's cottage, but it hardly mattered. The cold rushed over, past her. It didn't burrow under her skin.

Her legs seemed to grow longer as she ran, and around her the world was alive with scent and sound, a whole new map of experience. She dropped to all fours and shrugged herself out of the strange material that hindered her, nipping and gnawing until she'd worked herself free of the human clothing. A thin noose tightened around her throat, half choking her, and then the pain snapped away, and a silver chain slipped through her fur.

The abandoned clothes made a sad, unnatural puddle of color on the ground. A small bright chunk of silver blinked up from the nest of clothes. Sarah sniffed once, then sneezed. It all smelled of girl, and of things she didn't understand. There was the smell of a cottage and wood smoke, and for a moment she remembered the fire-bright warmth, the flashing white teeth of a smile, a promise. A boy's voice as dark and wild as the forest around her, like he was part of it, its spirit.

He'd given her warm tea sweetened with condensed milk. He'd wrapped a blanket around her shoulders when she was shivering and ill. He'd made a place for her when no one else wanted to. The thought of the boy with curling hair and kindness sent another shooting pain down her spine, and she screamed.

Howled.

The last of her girl-thoughts slipped away. A more interesting scent flashed across the air: a high spike of nervous terror, and under it the wine-warm curl of racing blood. Sarah raised her head and grinned, tasting the cold and the greeny-wet of the forest against her tongue, and there—the scent of the horned buck. It was close.

A flicker. A flash of white tail.

With a silent laugh, Sarah gave chase.

The forest became a living current around her, and she slipped through it as easily as a shark moving through the ocean. Fingers of leaves brushed against her coat, and the smell of the buck's terror was ripe and sharp ahead, leading her on. She hunted through the trees, and beneath her paws the ground turned again to cold dead needles, and the trees bowed under the weight of their white cloaks.

Still the buck stayed far ahead, bounding always just out of reach. A shadow appeared at Sarah's side, breath rasping, eyes wide and tongue lolling. A beast, like her. It was far bigger, and it ran without flagging, mirroring her every twist and turn.

Sarah's breath burned against her ribs, her paws ached. The buck ran. The shadow-beast next to Sarah began to draw ahead until finally, utterly exhausted, Sarah stumbled and collapsed, her sides shuddering, steam rising from her coat and panting tongue.

The ground was cold against her belly, almost soothing, and Sarah stretched out, trying to cool her overheated limbs. She was certain that she'd never stand again, that she'd lie there forever.

A spiral of snow fell from one of the higher branches and settled on her coat, glistening there for a moment before melting. She closed her eyes and waited. The snow would eventually cover her, and that would be her cold and quiet grave.

Even as a beast, Sarah felt calmed by the thought. There was something very appealing about drifting away here, just forgetting and being forgotten.

There was no need to be a girl again. To move again.

A slight change in the air made her shudder. Something was there, watching her. She could feel it. With an immense effort she opened one eye. Standing downwind was the buck. It stepped out of the wreath of leaves and closer to her. The horns were lyre shaped, like a delicate crown.

Sarah growled, but the buck merely walked a little closer, pointed cloven hooves picking delicately as it made its way toward her. When it was standing right over her body, it shook its head once, and the shiver traveled down its body, shaking its skin from its bones like a fine mist.

In its place stood a boy. A familiar boy, who smelled of fires and pines. He crouched down, put one hand between her ears, and gently scratched. He didn't talk, just comforted her like she was nothing more than a large dog, tired out from a run.

He stood and clicked his tongue. "Sarah," he said.

The name drifted through her head, fine as smoke. It was hers, she was sure of it.

"Sarah, *remember.*"

She did. Little things, snatches of her past. She was not only a beast, but something else too.

"You dropped this," the boy said. From his hand dangled a fine silver chain, with a small charm weighting it. A bear.

Sarahbear. She had a mother and a father, and . . . there were others, people and beasts and some who were neither. With a massive sigh, Sarah clambered to her paws. Her legs were shaky; her head felt weighted down by the budding spikes of her horns. They were little more than nubs, not big enough yet to curl like her grandfather's or the other beast's, but still they seemed far too heavy.

"It's a long walk back," Alan said softly. "We'll take it slow."

Sarah was so exhausted that her head hung, her back legs kept collapsing under her. The heat of her hunt slowly left her, and she began to shake from the cold, and from an exhaustion so complete that all she wanted to do was curl up and die.

She was faintly aware of Alan pausing to gather some bright scraps of clothing, muddy and wet, from the ground, but otherwise the journey back to the cottage passed in a shuddering, disjointed dream. All she knew, the only thing that kept her walking, was a desire to keep to the boy's side. She felt that there was some connection between them, and that if she stopped, she would never know what it was.

She would be lost.

14

HUNTING THE WREN

FINALLY THE COTTAGE came into view, and Sarah followed Alan inside.

"Wait there," he said, pointing to the kitchen. She dripped miserably on the flagstones, while Alan went to feed the dying coals in the grate. Once he had gotten the fire going and thrown an old threadbare towel before it, he nodded to her. "Lie down, then. Get warm."

She slunk over to the fire and collapsed before the black iron of the grating. The heat blasted across her, and the room filled with the smell of drying fur and pine gum.

"Sleep," Alan told her. Behind her, he was making himself another cup of tea, and the sharp burn of the brandy cut cleanly through all the other smells.

Sarah sneezed and flopped her head back down. Sleep sounded good.

"We'll talk in the morning," Alan said. His voice drifted over her, the words settling like leaves.

She gave a *hmph* in answer.

"I'll talk, I suppose—you'll just have to listen until you find your words again," he said. "You're being very inconvenient," Alan added softly.

His fingers dug gently behind her ears, scratching the thin fur around the nubs of her horns. Alan sighed, and Sarah sighed with him, a deep groan of agreement, before the warmth settled into her bones and dragged her to sleep.

✦┼ ──❖┈❖── ┼✦

Sarah woke to lazy silence. There was a distant bird call, and the ever-present whispersong of the trees, but other than that she could hear nothing. She stretched out, half wondering where she was and why she was lying on the floor.

She froze.

Her hands were covered in thick brindled fur, and each stumpy finger ended in a curved claw, dark brown as bitter chocolate.

"What?" she said, only it came out in a yelp. She scrambled up onto all fours and shook her head furiously. When that made no difference, she screamed. It was a thundering howl, wilder and stranger than any animal noise she'd ever heard before.

Stop. She snapped her jaws shut and breathed heavily, her flanks trembling.

A sea of images washed over her: a hunt, a race through

✦┼ 163 ┼✦

the forest after a buck that was not a buck. Of another beast at her side, of failure, of a jumble of scents and animal thoughts that felt more like pictures made of smells and falls of light than actual thoughts.

Last night I turned into a beast, she thought. The words were clear among the dizzying memories of the hunt. *Today I can think like a human.* Her breathing slowed and she turned, looking about her from this new perspective. The cottage smelled safe and familiar, of tea and wood smoke and moss and nettles and Alan.

Alan. Sarah dropped her head and whined. *This is his fault.* A twist tore through her, an ache so awful and splendid that she was ready to collapse onto the ash-streaked rug and sob.

If beasts can even cry, which I doubt. She raised her head again and made a soft sound, halfway between a gruff bark and a human laugh. *But they can speak. Or at least Grandfather can, so I need to remember how.*

Her ears lifted, and the hackles along her back raised in slow motion. Someone was walking toward the cottage, the grass brushing at his legs. Not someone—even if she couldn't hear from the tread, Sarah would have known anyway. She turned and sat down to stare at the door, waiting for him.

"Ah," Alan said when he opened the door to find her glaring in his direction. "Awake, are you?" He had a brace of rabbits slung over one shoulder, and the smell of them was almost overwhelming. Meat and blood and fur, and the last lingering trace of ice.

Sarah felt the saliva pooling in her mouth, and shook her head. She'd save the drooling on the floor for when he wasn't looking. Instead she growled at him, her jaw wrinkling up around her teeth.

"It's not my fault you've gone and turned," Alan said. "Besides, these are for you." He lifted the rabbits from his shoulder and held them out. Their dark eyes looked like black marbles, though the shine was already drying off them.

But it is your fault, Sarah thought. *Even if you don't know it. Actually, it's worse that you don't know it.*

She'd felt it. The moment that her casual liking for Alan had slipped into stranger waters. One moment he'd been interesting and improbable, and the next . . .

It had been like the world twisted off its axis, reinvented itself.

And she'd turned.

She wondered if her father had known about how the curse was triggered. Sarah remembered when she was younger, how her parents would laugh about falling in love at the same moment, as if joking about their ridiculous romance would take some of the fairy-tale sugar off it and make it palatable to others.

Except maybe that hadn't been it at all. Maybe they had laughed because they knew, and if they hadn't laughed they would have cried.

Sarah took a deep shuddering breath and made herself look squarely at Alan. Nothing about him had changed. He was the same lanky, underfed young man with dirty feet, and hair that curled and tangled. And yet somehow it seemed that the light hit him differently, made him impossible to stare at for too long, made him unreal, untouchable.

He'd been a buck. In the forest, he'd been a crowned buck on long graceful legs, and he'd outrun her.

No. It's all just the confusion from last night. She lowered her nose and whined.

"Your words will come back," Alan said. "Don't you worry. But you are eating these outside." He tossed the rabbits through the door. They landed in the grass with two thumps. "Go on, then. I want breakfast too, girl."

Hunger prodded Sarah out the door, and she nosed her way to where the two rabbits lay, legs akimbo. The wind plucked at the pale fur on their bellies. For now, they were still limp and warm, but it wouldn't be long before they turned stiff, and the last of the blood-heat leached out into the ground.

Ugh. I'm not eating that. But the smell that rose from them was more appetizing than any of Nanna's stews. And she was ravenous from the fruitless hunt, and the change. Animal instinct kicked in, swallowing up the human thoughts. She dragged the first corpse into a secluded part of the little meadow, and set to breakfast.

+⊱ ⟶⊙⟵ ⊰+

She was gnawing on the last of the bones when Alan came across the clearing toward where she was lying.

"Got your voice back yet?" He stopped a few feet away and squinted at her. "We're going to have to find Freya," he said. "You understand that, right? Wherever she's gotten to, we need to speak to her."

Sarah whined. It was more important than ever that she convince Freya to tell her how to break the curse. It wasn't just her grandfather and her father who were beasts; she'd been caught in the snare too. There were other beasts in the forest, racing between the trees, smelling the blood in the cold air, and already she'd taken a step closer to losing what was left of her humanity, had let herself get caught up in the pull of the chase, the urge to kill. She'd hunted with one of them last night—

"Beast!" she yelped.

"I'm not blind," Alan said.

"No. Beast. Other. Who?"

He narrowed his eyes. "You know who. Doesn't make him safe. He's lost her, and it's driven him mad. He doesn't even think like people anymore. It's a good thing he left you with your grandmother when he did."

"No," Sarah said. She'd known. In her heart of hearts, of course she'd known; she'd just never wanted to accept that the mindless animal in the forest was all that was left of her father.

Alan dropped to a crouch, bringing his face level with hers. Even now, with her worry and her loss climbing over her like fleas, she found his face too bright to look at. "You can't help him. He's looking for her, and that's all he cares about."

"Hunt?"

Alan nodded.

And if he caught her mother, the wren-woman . . . Sarah shuddered. "Find. Bird."

"What?" A frown pinched at his forehead, and his amber eyes darkened.

"Moth. Er. Find first."

"It's not that easy," Alan said. "I've been looking for her, and here I am." He spread his hands, showing the empty palms. "But," he said, his voice slowing, his frown deepening, "you could help."

"Yes." A shivery thrill danced down her spine and set her tail thumping against the earth. "Yes. Find." She raised her head, eyes closed, and thought of the smell of her mother, that scent of lilies and vanilla, of starlight and hot chocolate. The sound of her voice singing cradle songs and lullabies, soft and weak and off-key. A beautiful sound, to Sarah. It was there, a memory made real. A connection that only they had. It was a bond she had to use before she lost herself entirely to being a beast. "Can find," she said.

"And you think you can get to her first?" Alan stood, shrugging his shoulders like a great burden had just been lifted from him. "Before your father?" For a moment, Sarah let herself look at him properly. It hurt, but she stood firm, eyes unblinking.

The curse said that she would be saved only if the person she loved fell in love with her. Alan wasn't going to do that—he thought she was only a child. And worse, now a child who was mostly not even human.

It was love that cursed, and love that saved.

So, what if she could make herself fall out of love with him? It didn't matter that he was kind, that he'd looked after her when no one else would—there had to be something else, something that could make her hate him. He was unpredictable; he was magic and strange. He was probably lying to her about *something*.

It didn't help. She concentrated on his physical flaws, on

the skewed incisors that twisted his smile off balance, the size of his ears. His chin was too small and his mouth too wide. Taken separately, every feature was wrong. Unfortunately, together they made Alan, which wasn't helping. Sarah growled and shook her head.

He was older than she was, perhaps by hundreds of years. Time in the forest was always shifting. It meant nothing. It meant everything.

"Find her, girl. And we can maybe save one life." Alan looked past her, toward the forest. "And that'll be something, at least. Almost as good as breaking a curse." He looked suddenly contrite. "We'll find something to fix you," he said. "I'll make certain of it. Freya will help you. I know how to make her change her mind. How to get her on my side."

Sarah felt her heart step out of time and discovered, with a mixture of relief and despair, that beasts couldn't cry.

✦┤───→··←───┤✦

They'd been wandering the forest for hours. Occasionally Sarah caught a delicious curl of a familiar smell, but the scents were faded, and the trails always seemed to end in nothingness, doubled back on themselves.

Alan said nothing about her failure as he plodded behind her.

A musky beast-note came strongly from the east, and Sarah sneezed, backing up the trail they were on.

"And?" he asked, finally shaken out of his silence.

"Beast," said Sarah.

"What about her? Your mother?"

Sarah shook her head and tasted the air again. The frustrating thing was that the memory-smell of her mother was everywhere. And if she pricked her ears, she could hear her voice, sounding like it did when Sarah had put her ears underwater when she was younger and listened to the indistinct sound of her parents' conversations through the pipes and walls. Her voice ran under the forest ground, through the leaves and the pine needles. It was in the wind. It came from everywhere and so was nowhere. "Can smell. Can hear," she said. "Can't find."

"Well, tell me what she was like—the things that made her happy."

"Warm," Sarah said, then sat down to ponder. Anything: her favorite colors, the food she'd liked. But all those details had slipped away. Even her face had become doll-like and unreal. She knew her mother's eyes had been brown, but she couldn't picture them. She'd worn yellow dresses in the summer and red ones in the winter. And always, she'd looked like the warmest thing in the world. Red, and yellow, and then at the end when she'd stopped being in love, she'd dulled into nothing-colors. Had worn a coat of winter blue that washed her pale.

She'd been angry and sad, and her songs had changed. She'd listened to old radio stations that played music by dead singers. She'd started going outside to stare at the sun and hold cigarettes that she hardly smoked.

Maybe that was why it was so hard for Sarah to picture her mother—she'd never been sure which of them was the real one.

Except for arum lilies. Her mother had always liked those, no matter what persona she'd been wearing. And she'd liked bees. Sarah remembered how her mother would always rescue bees from pools. That had never changed.

Sarah pricked her ears, stilled, and waited. Her mother would be with the bees, with the lilies. She wouldn't be here in the forest. This was her father's realm—and hers now, she supposed.

Sarah turned her face, feeling the sun pull her. Even though it barely dripped through the leaves, and when it did its light was muted and green, the sun called her, and Sarah knew where to go.

The light drew her back, away from the cold heart of the forest and the icy pull of the Within where the witches used to live, back to the castle.

The woods bowed out of her way, and the drone of bees vibrated the air. A sound she was so used to ignoring, and now it had become the most important thing in her world.

"You're sure you're going the right way?" Alan drawled.

Sarah huffed once without looking back at him, and walked faster.

The last of the trees gave way, and there before her stood the crumbling remains of Nanna's castle. The grass grew dark and wiry, but it was spotted here and there with little dark blue flowers like sleeping stars. Sarah trotted out along the widening path toward the vegetable garden with its low, crumbling wall and the damp shadows where the lilies clumped together, showing their regal white trumpets and long yellow tongues. Their season was long over, but here they stayed, even though their edges were withering brown.

The lilies.

And the bees.

"Here," said Sarah, and wondered why she hadn't realized it before. That her mother had been here, watching her. Perhaps, even as a bird, there'd been some last thread of mothering instinct that had tied her to wherever Sarah was. She breathed in deeply, and there it was, stronger than ever, an elusive smell on the air. Not perfumes or memories of meals and blankets, but a taste of salt and human sorrow.

Sarah sat patiently, and closed her eyes against the thin sun. The bees droned louder, the doves purred liquidly from the treetops. It wasn't them she was interested in.

It came softly across the grass, dancing with the hum of wings. A small sound. Her heart beat faster, blood thrumming in her ears. She could feel every shift of the world against her fur, each slight change in the wind, she could feel the earth spinning beneath her paws, the roots of dandelions and aspens alike, threading through the mantle of soil.

Even wings of small creatures change the shape of the universe, Sarah understood suddenly. She didn't have to go hunt her mother down—not like Alan did, not like her father. Her mother's love for her was still there, sleeping under her skin.

All she had to do was be still, and to understand how the forest worked. It gave you what you wanted, whether you knew you wanted it or not. "Mother," she said, her voice almost human.

The bird flew across the clearing.

Even with her eyes still closed, Sarah knew. She felt the

passing of its shadow, could smell feathers and hear the thrum of its heart. She felt it land before her, tiny claws pricking at the world-skin.

Sarah opened her eyes and looked down.

The bird really was small, just *so big*, no larger than could fit in a palm. It was plain and brown. It could have been any of a thousand birds, nondescript, nothing. It watched her with its beady eyes, and the last bit of magic holding the miasma of memory around it finally left.

Alan moved so quickly that Sarah didn't even have time to blink. One moment, the bird that had been her mother was hopping on the ground before her, and the next, it was cupped in his hands like a dark secret.

The bird was just a bird now. The last of the magic that had tied the bird to her was broken. Sarah could feel the loss of her mother inside her, like a hand twisting out her organs, rearranging them to fill the missing spaces.

Alan ignored her. "Freya," he yelled to the castle ruins, but there was no sign of any of the inhabitants. He called her name again. "Come to me," he yelled, and held one hand high. "I have her, Freya. Come to me."

Even Sarah, who was not being commanded to do anything, could feel the power behind his words. He was stronger than she'd realized.

A white shimmer swept out from over the forest, and the raven fell toward them like a hurled stone. She landed on the bare soil before Sarah's paws. The white bird looked to Sarah and shook her head. "I thought you safe still. You were too young."

"Freya," Alan said again, and the raven finally turned her attention to him.

"Beastkeeper," she said. "A loyal boy, but foolish. You should have gone back to the city and left your love for the forest behind."

"I couldn't," he said. "You had made me too much a part of the land by the time Inga cursed you."

The raven nodded. "I saw, but I hoped that with me gone, you would find your way back to being human. There was none of my magic to keep you here."

"You were wrong," said Alan.

"I always was." She hopped forward. "You did this to the girl?"

Alan looked over at Sarah. He'd known why she'd changed. She could see it in his eyes. He'd always known. It felt like being drowned, like seeing the last of hope slipping away like tiny silvery bubbles of breath.

"It wasn't meant to happen that way. I befriended her, but I didn't expect—" He shook his head. "I needed her," he said. "I needed her to find the wren."

"For what?" the raven said, and Sarah was glad the raven had asked, because her own words were stuck deep inside her now, the last gasps of air she could not let go.

"This," Alan said, and raised two of his fingers, enough that the little wren could struggle its head free. "I've come to free you," he said, and twisted his hands just so.

15

TOWARD THE WITHIN

THE RAVEN WAS WRONG. Falling out of love was not always a slow descent, too dull for stories. Sarah fell out of love as quickly as the snap of a neck.

The raven cawed, but that was the final harsh note it made. A high screaming filled Sarah's ears, a howl of wind and beast. The air froze around them, and in one moment, the world turned from fading warmth to the bitter snowstorm fury of the Within, freed now as its ruler was.

The scream went on forever, a kettle that never stopped boiling. Sarah couldn't move for the pain of it; the sound dug needles into her head. She curled up, trying to protect herself from the raging storm, from the razor shards of ice blown around her.

And then it stopped.

A sudden silence, no movement. She raised her head warily, and saw a world frozen in time. The ice and snow hung in the air as if held by invisible wires. They twirled in place, scattering light between their thousand broken crystals. At the center of the motionless maelstrom stood two figures.

Alan, with his offering held out before him, its neck limp.

And the witch. Freya. The other grandmother. She wasn't pretty or terrible. A handsome woman. Ugly-beautiful, with proud eyes. She was wearing a cloak of white feathers that pooled heavily about her feet. Her hair was silver with age, but her face was unlined, her eyes the pale blue of a winter sky. All about her hung a feeling of immense power.

It pressed Sarah down, held her in her place.

Then Freya spoke. Her voice was no louder than the softest hush of a playful wind against the very tops of trees, but at the same time, it was loud enough to shake the bones of the world. "What have you done?" she asked, staring at the boy, and at the dead bird in his hands.

"Freed you," Alan said, and let the bird drop. "Because you wouldn't do it yourself."

"I would have stayed cursed," said Freya. She did not look down at the little corpse at her feet. "I would have stayed cursed."

Alan swallowed, his Adam's apple bobbing. "She was dead anyway, the moment she left him. You know that. She couldn't live unless you lifted the curse from them all. And you never would because it would cost you all you are." He held his ground, eyes like suns. "If you'd loved her like you said, you would have set her free no matter what. She was already dead. Your curse did that. *You* did that."

"I could not lift it." Freya stepped forward, breaking the spell that held the world still. The ice crystals dropped to the ground, covering it in a sea of shattered glass.

Sarah tensed, feeling herself rise with the release of the pressure. She wanted to tear Alan's throat out. She wanted to make him run.

And then I will be nothing more than a beast, truly. The curse was far from broken. She still had to hold on to what was left of the human parts of her. The struggle was immense. Froth built up in her mouth and dripped from her jaws with the effort of keeping herself from leaping up at him, from feeling his windpipe crushed between her teeth. Instead, she looked at her grandmother's feet, at the dead bird there. It was just a bird, as Alan said.

It had stopped being her mother the day it flew from her life.

The truth of it didn't make things better.

"I did what I had to," Alan said. "I only did the things you should have. It was that, or leave you to die a slave to your own hatred."

Freya put her hand to Alan's cheek. "So loyal, after all these years. And all done to free me." She slid her hand back into his hair, and tightened her grip. "Did you think I would be pleased?"

"Yes," he said, but it came out a hiss of pain. "I gave you back to yourself, returned all your power."

"She was my daughter." Freya glanced down at Sarah. "My

granddaughter is a beast now, her life ruined, and what did you do in exchange? Hunted down one little bird and snapped its neck."

"One little bird who never loved you," Alan said. His eyes were streaming, but he kept his voice even, low. As if he was trying to calm the very different beast that Freya had become.

"I had a selfish daughter, a flighty daughter, a daughter who changed her heart as easily as her outfits." Freya smiled, showing her teeth unnaturally. "I did not need a beastkeeper to remind me of that. Still." She released Alan. "I suppose I owe you some small reward, at least."

Alan looked away for the first time. "I want nothing from you, just for you to be free. Before you took me in, I was nothing more than a starveling child with a dead family. I owe you at least a life."

"I should have left you where I found you."

"But you didn't."

The silence streamed between them, and Sarah concentrated, trying to piece together these last bits of Alan's and her grandmother's story—a chance bit of compassion, and this was what had come of it.

"I didn't save you out of pity, boy. I needed a beastkeeper, nothing more. And now you think to repay my thoughtless kindness with some of your own. How noble you think you are," Freya said. "Fine, then. You've freed me from my curse. Ask for one thing. Contracts are contracts."

"Change the girl back," he said.

Sarah's heart leaped up, beating against her rib cage.

"I cannot," said Freya. "You stupid, stupid child." She

moved forward, her arms lifting the white cloak of feathers around her, and embraced Alan.

The storm rose as suddenly as it had stopped; a brief roar of icy wind passed through the clearing and was gone again.

And Freya and Alan were gone with it.

◦┊——◦❯┄◦❮——┊◦

The birds in the forest boughs resumed their song as if nothing had happened. The ice was already melting into the ground; the bees began their relentless drone.

A small breeze ruffled the feathers on the wren. It lay in a puddle of ice water. Sarah shuffled closer and picked up the body as carefully as she could with her sharp teeth, not wanting to break any more bones, even now.

From the castle came a bang as the doors crashed open. Nanna stood outlined in the castle mouth, like the start of a scream. "Where is she?" Nanna said. Her eyes narrowed as she took in the animal standing in the clearing and realized it was Sarah. "And you too, now," she said. "Well, I suppose there's a certain irony to that."

Her eyes went to the little corpse Sarah held so tenderly.

"What have you done? You've set Freya free, you ungrateful little wretch!" She spread her arms, her cloak of fur flapping heavily behind her, and a raking wind sprang up around Sarah, furnace hot, clawing at her eyes and mouth and nose. The wind tugged at her fur with cruel fingers, dragging her across the earth toward her grandmother. "First him, and now this?" Nanna's screech was as rabid and fierce as the wind itself. "For this, girl, you will suffer. I'll see to it."

Sarah shook the magic off with a huge burst of will, and tried to run. She needed to be far from the castle and from Nanna's sphere of power. The falling-down turrets and the broken walls overrun with nettles were all that was left of Nanna's magic. Freya had told her that Nanna's power didn't extend all the way to the river. If she could get there, she would be safe, at least.

She strained against the pulling wind, head bowed as she struggled to take one step after the other toward the forest. It was not safe either, not at all, but it seemed now that nowhere was safe. The people who should have loved her hadn't; her enemies wore smiles, and her family, snarls.

The wind released her as her grandmother's burst of power faltered, and finally Sarah leaped free, galloping for the cool dark of the shadowed forest.

If nothing else, now that she was a beast, the forest accepted her completely. Sarah raced through the twisting deer trails, following the secret magic of the ancient land. *It is an old forest,* Alan had said, *and old forests remember.* He had shown her how to do this, but it had seemed strange and unbelievable to her—certainly not something she'd ever be able to do herself. But now, as a beast, the woods flowed around her, dragging her on. Now she understood—it was about being one with the forest, and as a human girl, she'd never been able to do it.

The bird was warm in her mouth, and Sarah had to fight against the urge to crunch down and swallow it. *Don't. Don't think about it.* Instead, she let the trees and the branches open before her and show her where they wanted her to be.

She was far from the castle now, but still going in aimless circles.

The magic of witches and humans and curses had failed her completely. It was time to trust something older. She held on to the tiny bit of humanity she had left and gave up the rest of herself to being a beast.

It felt like letting go of a balloon. The little speck of her that was a girl who liked to read, who missed her mother, drifted away until it was lost in the sky. It became easier to race through the darkening boughs. The trails widened and the forest led her on. Her paws did not break the fallen twigs, the way a girl's clumsy feet might, and the branches did not whip her cheeks or tangle in her fur. She felt no cold, just warmth and speed.

She was only vaguely aware when the second beast joined her again, and together they ran. This time there was no crowned buck to follow, no loyal, beautiful, cruel boy bound to the forest and to the shape of its magic. There was just the forest itself.

Another beast, older, greater than either of them, slipped from the darkness and became the head of their pack. His horns were sharper now, his fur longer, bright-washed by rain and snow. He ran silently with them.

Sarah felt the pack-rightness of her father alongside her, of her grandfather ahead, and redoubled her efforts, pounding her legs against the frozen ground. There was ice in her lungs, frost on her fur, and starlight-bright snow swirled around them. The trees were glass-coated. The forest was leading them to the Within. Sarah leaped ahead, knowing what she needed to do.

The river waited for them. The pathways had taken them to a bank that was less steep, where the rapids ran shallower, and a trail of rocks broke the surface like a bridge of old tusks. White water frothed about their roots. Sarah paused on the snow-deep bank and felt the cold wet her belly.

The other two beasts looked at her in concern. The older one howled mournfully and said nothing. The younger merely sat and said nothing. They wanted her to run away with them. They did not understand why she had brought them here to this terrible river.

They said nothing.

They told her this with their ears, their eyes, their whines and growls.

Even her grandfather had lost what was left of him here in the forest.

Sarah's legs were numb. The only warmth now seemed to come from the bird in her mouth. It was a coal against her tongue, and the urge to drop it and cool her burning jaw with mouthfuls of snow was strong.

Pain. Drop. Drop. Drink, the beast part of her mind clamored. It was a rage of instinct, but Sarah tightened her grip, clenching her teeth like a cage around the coal-burn of her mother's body.

My name is Sarah. My mother's name is Merete. Her mother's name is Freya. We have not always been beasts. She turned to the huge shadowy figures. *My name is Sarah. My father's name is Leon. My grandfather had a name once: Eduard. We have not always been beasts.*

Her father's eyes were animal, with not a flicker of human

understanding anywhere in them. He had run with her because he sensed pack-rightness, nothing more. He had no words; he had lost his love, and himself. He whined, turning away from the raging waters and disappearing back between the long trunks of the pine trees.

Her grandfather watched her as if deep inside him a little part still understood what she was doing and why, but he made no move to go with her.

Turn back, and be a beast complete, or go on and do this one last human thing. Sarah looked at the raging waters. Perhaps it would be better if she just followed them, after all.

Her heart tightened as if an invisible fist had closed around it, and Sarah whined softly. She held the burning body firmly in her mouth and took an awkward leap to the nearest wet-black rock. It was slippery as eel skin, and she scrabbled there, her claws splayed for a better grip. Water splashed against her, drenching what little fur had stayed dry this far. She was bedraggled, the wet fur clinging to her skin. She felt smaller and weaker.

The next few stones were easy enough. They lay close together, and with slow, careful movements, she inched her way toward the center of the river. The water ran black, shadows of deep green flickering below her. Sarah hung in place. The distance to the next rock was too far for a simple jump. Even as a beast, she wasn't sure she would make it. Her heart was hammering as she looked back to see if her grandfather was following.

The bank was spotted with her paw prints. The large beast still sat, watching her progress. His black horns rose in high coils behind his ears, and for a moment, he looked like something that wasn't flesh and bone and fur, but a shadowy nightmare creature. He raised his blunt head and howled once, a sound that set the trees to shivering, their snow loads dropping from them like falling cloaks. Then he turned and walked back into the forest.

The knowledge that even her grandfather had given up hit Sarah so hard that she almost lost her balance. Her back legs slipped into the water, and she scratched and wriggled, trying to get a grip on the black stone and pull herself up out of the freezing current.

Finally, she had all four paws back on her outcrop. Her soaked fur provided no protection from the cold now. She shook, only her fierce determination keeping her from just letting go and falling to the water and allowing it to take her away. She knew she wasn't going to make that leap to the next rock, but she gathered her paws under her, crouching down and preparing her hind legs like springs. The rock wavered in her sight. *A beast would give up. A beast would go back to the woods and forget this.*

She jumped. The water tore and roared beneath her, and her brief flight ended in a splash that almost made her drop the burden she carried. The current pulled her away from the rock, downstream.

Swim, Sarah commanded herself, and her legs obeyed, kicking out, kicking her toward the far bank, cold and white and waiting.

She lost track of all thought, counting out each kick, each paddle, until finally her forepaws made contact with the ice-crackled edges of the river, and she broke through them like finest glass, to drag herself shivering onto the snow-covered bank.

She stayed there, and a lethargic heat began to slowly replace the numb cold burn in her legs. A last shudder rippled through her exhausted body. Snow was still falling, and it made for her a white duvet. Sarah grinned mirthlessly. It was like being tucked up for bedtime, feeling the cool bed suck up her body heat and return it to her. A nest.

It would have all been fine, she could have stayed there and gone to sleep warm and safe. If it wasn't for the thing in her mouth.

Hot thing.

Drop. Her jaws worked, thick ribbons of spit dripped from them as she tried to work the burning thing out of her mouth.

She couldn't remember why she was carrying it. *Drop. Sleep.*

The beast that had been Sarah paused. It had been doing something, it knew. Someone had wanted it to take the burning thing. It struggled to its feet, shaking off the thin layer of snow. Its legs were trembling. *On,* said a voice in the back of its head. A clear voice. A human voice. *My name is Sarah. My mother's name is Merete. My grandmother's name is Freya. We—are—not—beasts.*

The beast struggled up the bank and made for the line of trees, deeper into the Within. No birds called here, and the winds ripped and tore, rising with every step the beast took closer to the last boundary.

The trunks rose to meet the beast and thickened, joined, until they had created a solid wall. It was higher than the castle towers, and the snow slammed against its smooth black surface to fall in drifts.

The beast raised one paw to claw against the wall. It could not open its mouth to speak, and all it knew was what the voice in its head was repeating endlessly.

My name is Sarah. My mother's name is Merete. My grand-mother's name is Freya. We are not beasts.

Not yet.

It dropped down, finally unable to move onward. The wall was colder even than the ice and snow, and it fizzed and hissed with magic. The beast pressed its burned mouth against the slick black surface, and let the corpse drop. It lay at the foot of the wall, small and perfect. It looked like at any moment it would leap back to its feet and hop about in the snow, bright-eyed, before it took wing,

The beast stared at the bird, and when it spoke, it had found the words.

"My name is Sarah, and I am not a beast."

With a terrible creaking sound, the wall began to tear. The split crackled down like an arrow point, to end at Sarah's paws. The gap it made was narrow, but on the other side stood the Within.

It was green and smelled of apples, and the air hummed.

Sarah bowed her head to gently lift the small corpse, then clambered up to squeeze through the rift in the wall.

16

THE WAY WE END

THE WITHIN WAS FULL of paths leading under tree boughs that turned from blossom to green leaf to golden apple to black and back again. With every step, the trees changed, shifting between seasons like dancers. White blossoms fell before Sarah's paws, and brown leaves, and withered fruit, but Sarah didn't hesitate. She kept her head down and walked on to the very heart of her grandmother's realm.

A single giant tree stood there, hollow but still living, its heavily laden branches held up by weathered posts. A green lawn dotted with small blue flowers made a carpet around it, and Freya, in her cloak of white feathers, sat on a chair under the shade of the branches. The chair could have been carved from rock, but was hidden beneath a layer of moss so green and deep it was hard to tell the original material of her throne.

Alan sat cross-legged at her feet, his hands in his lap. He was staring out into nothing. Where his amber eyes had been were empty hollows, the skin sewn closed. He turned his head as Sarah approached, tilting to hear her better. Around his neck was a fine silver chain, with a little silver bear pendant.

Freya made no move as Sarah padded closer; her expression was set in blank misery.

When Sarah was only a few feet from her grandmother's throne, she dropped the bird. It lay between them.

"I cannot help you," Freya said. "The terms of the curse are as they are."

"I know," said Sarah. "I think I understand now. The curse can only end with your death." She shrugged. "The curse will end anyway."

"How?"

"After me, there will be no more human children to grow up and fall in love with anyone. Nanna has gone mad. Grandfather and my dad are only animals." The words were hard to speak. Sarah had to say them slowly and carefully, thinking each sound out before she said it. The hardest were still to come. She raised her snout and stared into Freya's storm-eyes. "And my mother is dead."

Sarah shuffled back a little, to get a better look at Alan. Freya had blinded him, but it seemed that even so, she couldn't bring herself to destroy him. Just as Sarah couldn't now.

He'd tried to save them, after all. In his own way.

"So I brought her here," Sarah said, and pointed her

muzzle at the bird. "We should bury her properly, and then when that's done, I will go back to the forest."

"And forget?" said Freya.

Sarah nodded. "You told me yourself that curses always go in circles. I am choosing to step out of the circle. Maybe I can't break it, but I can refuse to be a part of it, to step away from revenge and jealousy." She looked her grandmother squarely in the face. "I can do what you couldn't. I can forgive."

"You say that because you're a child, you think it's simple—"

Sarah ignored her. "I forgive you," she said softly, "and I forgive him." She glanced at Alan. It was hard, yes, but somehow easier than she'd expected, once the words were out. Perhaps it was this, more than remembering her name, that made her truly human.

There was a long moment of silence as Freya considered her. "There are days . . ." she said, and laughed bitterly. "Almost every day, if we are to be honest, now, at the end of it—almost every day I wish I had never met Inga. I cursed her because she couldn't see what I wanted her to see. And I cursed Eduard because he was handsome, and vain." She stood, and walked down from her stone chair to lift up the little bird.

When Sarah had entered the Within, the corpse had stopped blistering her mouth. It was nothing more than a simple dead bird.

Freya held it in her palms and pressed her mouth to the feathers. "And look what it brought me," she said softly.

"You can break the curse," Alan said.

Freya snorted in disgust. "I cannot," she said. "I am the witch of the Within, the most powerful of my kind, and I *will* not."

"You could pass your power on." Alan turned his blind face away from them both, as if even now he couldn't bear to look at the scene before him. "You know that as well as I do."

"Ah," said Freya softly. "And you think you should be the recipient, beastkeeper?"

"It's amazing the things you learn when you start listening to the forest," Alan said. "You're the witch of the woods, true enough, and the woods are endless and ageless, but you're not the first, nor will you be the last."

"Is he right?" Sarah growled. "Could you have ended it all?"

"It's not that simple," said Freya. "The power that you think I can so simply *transfer*, as if it were a rubied crown, or a title—it is the only thing that keeps me alive." She drew her cloak around her. "And even if I decided to simply walk to my own death, something could still go wrong. If the vessel I chose were too weak or flawed to hold my power, there would be magical backlash beyond imagining. The storm you saw when I was freed would be nothing more than the merest glimpse of what could happen."

"You had him," Sarah said, and looked to the blind boy. "You could have stopped it all, freed my mother and father, Nanna and Grandfather, everyone, if you'd given it up to him?" She lunged up, driving Freya back into her seat, pinning her in place with her heavy paws on the witch's chest. "But you didn't. For what?" she roared. "Give it up. Give it up now, or I will tear your throat out myself."

"You wouldn't."

"I've threatened you before," Sarah said, "and you were quite right: back then I didn't mean it. But I promise you now that things have very definitely changed." She closed her teeth around Freya's throat and held her. She felt the flesh moving under her teeth when Freya whispered.

"Even now, I am stronger than you could ever be. I could call down birds to tear your eyes out, I could raise storms that would strip the skin right off your bones—"

"So why don't you?" Sarah said, the words muffled. "Why. Don't. You."

"The same reason you will not close your teeth and tear out my throat." Freya began to laugh softly, breathlessly. "Or perhaps the only thing stopping you is fear. Kill me, and see what happens."

"No," Sarah said. She held on to the word *forgive*, and though it took every ounce of self-control she had, she managed to ease her jaws loose and step away from her grandmother. *I can do this.* "Alan?"

He shifted at the sound of her voice.

"Stand up and take hold of my fur." Sarah leaped down to stand next to him. He curled one hand in the ruff of her neck. The touch shocked through her. Not in a heart-fluttering, weak-at-the-knees kind of way, but with the knowledge that in his own fashion, Alan was as cursed by Freya as any of the rest of them had been. "Get on," she said, "and hold tight."

"What are you doing?" he said, but even so, he did as he

was told, clambering onto her back like she was some kind of strange, shaggy pony.

"Leaving," said Sarah. "And so are you. You did terrible things to save her. I brought her daughter back—I'm her own granddaughter, and still she won't do what she should have done in the first place."

"I cannot," Freya shrieked. She held one hand at her throat, but Sarah could see the little red points where her teeth had nicked the skin. She wondered if she should have done it. *No. This is why the curses never ended. Because they were all of them so desperate for revenge. I'll break it my own way.* Still, she hoped that Freya might yet change her mind. It wasn't that she wanted her grandmother to die—there had been enough death. She merely wanted everything settled and ended, with a happily-ever-after like when curses ended in fairy tales.

Except this wasn't a tale—or it was, but as Freya had said when she was still a raven, it was the part of the story no one liked to tell: the unhappily-ever-after.

Sarah walked carefully forward, closer to Freya, worried that Alan might lose his grip and fall, but he had a good seat and his fingers were buried deep in her fur. The woman shivered once as she approached, but otherwise she made no move. "You can," Sarah said to her. "You just won't. But it doesn't matter anymore. I'm not a beast, I'm just beast-shaped, and the rest of the forest is waiting for me."

She turned away from the throne of moss and the witch who occupied it, but she couldn't stop herself from glancing back. "You can keep your power, you can keep the Within, but the day you realize that what you want has cost you more than it's worth, you will know where to find us."

Freya watched her, thin-lipped and stone-faced.

"Now," Sarah said to Alan, "hold fast."

And she ran.

AFTER

IT WAS THE END OF SUMMER, when the leaves on the trees were just considering the approach of autumn, and the first few had already begun to curl and fall. The wind was rising, still playful but with the snick of winter in its jaws, when Freya left the Within.

Six years—or maybe six hundred, or maybe sixty—had passed since Sarah had run from the Within and set out to be as human a beast as she could manage. She lived near Alan's cottage in the woods, mainly to make sure he was coping with his blindness. For the most part, he did better than she'd expected. Perhaps, Sarah supposed, because he had always been magical—more than a simple beastkeeper.

Over time, Sarah had done her best to build ties to Nanna,

and while she still wasn't the most pleasant person to be around, Nanna had tried, in her own way, to make amends. The loss of all her family had changed her, made her small and broken. The last few years had been better for her, because Grandfather had taken to creeping out from the forest and taking tea at the castle. On some days he was even human, so Sarah figured that love was a fickle thing, and she left them to it.

The beast that had been her father hunted with her sometimes on moonlit nights, but mostly he kept himself to himself, and Sarah saw less of him as time passed. She was sad, in the beginning, but she understood. It seemed there was nothing human left in him at all.

And between themselves, she and Alan had worked out a comfortable sort of friendship, one that never got too close to dabbling in curses. It was safer that way.

Sarah was lying in a spot of autumnal sun, watching the last of the season's white butterflies tumbling about the hollyhocks, listening to Alan whistling from the cottage kitchen as he made tea (a cup for him, a bowl for her), when the weather turned, and a bitter wind blew Freya right into their meadow.

The cabbage-white butterflies froze in midflight and tumbled to the ground, their wings crisped with an edging of ice. Sarah shook her head and got to her feet.

"Call him," snapped Freya.

"Call him yourself," said Sarah.

"Neither of you needs to call me," Alan pointed out, as he came out of the cottage. "I'm blind, not deaf."

"You," said Freya, and before any of them could say another

word, she grabbed Alan's arm, catching him in a viselike grip. He didn't try to pull free, just stood very still, his head raised to show his throat, like an animal waiting to be slaughtered. He still wore Sarah's silver chain, and Sarah had never mentioned it, waiting to see if one day he would realize, would take it off and throw it away.

"Oh," said Sarah. "You've made up your mind, then?"

"I have had an eternity to stare at a grave, and to remember, and to regret. I have had time to think," Freya said. She closed her eyes, and magic bubbled under the witch's skin, crawling its way into Alan like a host of worms. He gasped, a small sound of muted pain and surprise. The ground shuddered, the trees stretching out with roots and branches as the power swept from Freya and into Alan. A soft roaring throb moved below them as the forest came under new stewardship, and all its ancient magic passed into Alan's care.

"Be better than I was," Freya said, her fingernails curling like claws into his arm. She looked to Sarah. "Maybe the girl can teach you." Then the witch let go, and dropped to the ground, white with frost.

Alan took a slow shuddering breath and shivered. He had been expecting death.

The forest went very still for a moment, and then the wind changed direction, and the power swept up from the earth, through the pads of her paws and up her bones, sparking from her fur like flashes of static electricity. Sarah felt the curse break like a strand of snapping hair. Her animal skin fell from her body, puddling about her like an abandoned winter coat. She looked at her feet, pale and narrow in the long grass, and smiled. She could feel the threads of the curse stretching out and breaking.

In the woods, a beast became a man, and in a castle, two people stared at each other over teacups and remembered being young once, and innocent. The autumn wind ruffled playfully against Sarah's skin, and she hugged herself. The beast-coat of long fur had been its own kind of blessing, but even as she watched, it was fading away, melting into the grass. *Clothes. Clothes would be a wonderful plan right about now.*

"You're human," Alan said. "I can sense it."

"Apparently," said Sarah.

"This calls for tea."

"I think you may be right."

"Yours is currently in a bowl," Alan said. "We should probably do something about that."

"Clothes first," said Sarah. "And then we have a grave to dig."

Together, the girl who used to be a beast and the boy who had become a wizard buried Freya. They patted down the soil, and Sarah put her palm over the hand of the new king of the forest. "Tea," she said, and helped him to his feet.

ACKNOWLEDGMENTS

Beastkeeper was born in a flurry. A wordstorm. And after the last vowels settled in drifts came the job of raising it to its full potential.

My many thanks to all the people who helped me grow the story into shape: Marieke Nijkamp, Nerine Dorman, Jennifer Crow, Frances Thorndike, Elizabeth Retief, and Suzie Townsend and the readers at New Leaf Literary and Media. Special thanks to my editor Noa Wheeler, who asks the wisest questions; to George Newman, who makes me look literate; and to Ashley Halsey and Béatrice Coron for the cover. To the circle of writers who have been my friends for A Very Long Time Indeed. Musers, thank you for being the weird bunch you are, for the inspiration and the late-night sanity check-ins. To Mom, Dad, Chevonne, and Wesley, thank you for being supportive and for being proud of my books. And to my favorite Brian, my favorite Noa, and my favorite Tanith in all the world, who put up with much strangeness while I write, I love you guys. I think I'll keep you.